BRIE'S SUBMISSION

Hope's First Christmas

Red Phoenix

Copyright © 2019 Red Phoenix
Print Edition
www.redphoenixauthor.com

Hope's First Christmas: Brie's Submission
19th Book of the Brie Series

Cover by Shanoff Designs
Formatted by BB Books
Phoenix symbol by Nicole Delfs

All rights reserved. Except as permitted under the U.S. Copyright Act of 1976, no part of this publication may be reproduced, distributed, or transmitted in any form or by any means, or stored in a database or retrieval system, without the prior written permission of the author.

Dedication

Experiencing the magic of Christmas through these characters has been wonderful fun.

I hope you agree!

I must thank my muses, because they were seriously on fire when it came to Kinky Eve. The scenes came so fast, I struggled to keep up. That's when you know you have something special as an author, and there are so many special moments in this story.

This book reminded me why I love the Christmas season.

To my wonderful muses who have carried me through a difficult time, I thank you from the bottom of my heart.

To my editor Kh Koehler, thanks for keeping up with the crazy amount of words and for helping get this book out just in time for Christmas.

To my betas: Becki, Brenda, Maryiln and Kathy - thank you for giving this book your time and love.

Thank you, Shaonoff Designs, for making this joyful cover.

And of course, I must thank MrRed - the love of my life. He was a trooper, encouraging me on to the finish with everything that was going on in our personal lives.

This book brought me great joy writing it.

I hope it does the same for you, my friends!

SIGN UP FOR MY NEWSLETTER HERE FOR THE LATEST RED PHOENIX UPDATES

SALES, GIVEAWAYS, NEW RELEASES, PREORDER LINKS, AND MORE!

SIGN UP HERE

REDPHOENIXAUTHOR.COM/NEWSLETTER-SIGNUP

CONTENTS

Her First Word 1
New Insight 15
A Confession 26
Ghost from the Past 36
Christmas Kittens 49
Kinky Eve 64
Holiday Scenes 80
Unexpected Surprises 103
Sexy Santa 117
Christmas Morn 133
Russian Gifts 146
A Gathering 160
Rumble in the Hills 178
Warm Afterglow 193
Coming Next 198
About the Author 199
Other Red Phoenix Books 202
Connect with Red on Substance B 207

Her First Word

Brie's heart started racing when she heard someone frantically pounding on the door. Then she heard the familiar accent of her favorite Russian as he called out, "Open up, *radost moya*!"

Rushing to the door, she swung it open and was shocked to see a giant pine tree on her front porch. "What's this?"

"It's a Christmas tree," Rytsar stated with a laugh as he carried the huge tree through the doorway with the help of his men and headed into the great room.

"You can't put that there, Rytsar! Sir hates Christmas trees."

"*Moye solntse* needs one."

Brie laughed, pointing at the miniature bonsai

tree with twinkly lights on the coffee table. "But we already have a tree."

He looked at it, snorting with amusement.

Rytsar's men had already set the tree into the stand they had brought and stood back. Rytsar pulled a switchblade from his back pocket and quickly cut the strings, unleashing the voluminous boughs.

Brie's eyes widened when she saw it fully unfurled and let out a gasp. "It's so huge…"

Rytsar smirked, nodding at the tree. "That's what she said."

Brie put her hands to her mouth, trying not to giggle.

He looked back at her confidently and winked.

"Sir isn't going to let this tree stay," she warned him.

Rytsar faced Brie, putting his hand over his heart. "I have not felt this kind of joy for Christmas in ages. My brother would not be so cruel as to rip it away from me over a simple pine tree."

Brie looked back at the giant tree. "There is nothing simple about that tree, Rytsar."

Shadow suddenly appeared and walked

straight up to it. After taking several sniffs of the lower boughs, he opened his mouth and pulled his lips back, making Brie laugh.

Apparently satisfied with the smell of the natural pine, Shadow disappeared under the boughs and proceeded to climb up the trunk, each limb shaking under his weight.

"Shadow…no!" Brie cried.

"Let him be," Rytsar assured her. "The tree is strong and the stand will hold."

Halfway up, Shadow settled on a branch and started purring as he looked at them from within the branches.

"Even the *kot* approves."

"I don't think Sir is going to care, no matter who likes it."

Rytsar grinned. "Maxim, get the ornaments."

"You bought ornaments, too? Okay, now you're just being cocky," Brie laughed.

"Just a few," he answered. "They are made of papier-mâché so that *moye solntse* and the *kot* cannot break them. The varnish used to protect them is safe for babies and pets."

"You're so thoughtful."

Maxim came back with a wooden box and handed it to Rytsar. He opened it and smiled as he picked up an ornament to show Brie.

"Rytsar…" she murmured in awe. "This is incredible."

Brie took the large egg with a winter scene of Russia painted on it. Looking closer she gasped. "Oh, my goodness! Is that my cabin?"

He grinned. "It is…"

Each ornament had a painted winter scene of Russia that Brie was personally familiar with, from the legendary Red Square and the iconic Saint Basil's Cathedral, to Rytsar's family's mansion and the modern skyline where Rytsar lived in his apartment in Moscow part of the year. Each scene brought back memories, but her favorite by far was the cabin by the lake. The tree where she'd been tied was painted prominently on the front of the ornament.

Brie looked at him. "I love them all."

He kissed her on the forehead before giving her the cabin ornament. "Hang it on the tree, *radost moya.*"

She almost felt naughty as she placed it on the tree, knowing how Sir would react when he saw this giant pine tree in their home. But, when she looked at the ornament hanging on the bough, her heart was filled with joy.

She loved Christmas! This was her favorite time of the year, even though she knew Sir didn't care for the holiday.

Brie heard Hope wake up from her nap and went to get her. While she was walking back with Hope in her arms, she heard Sir return home.

In a voice loud and clear, he stated, "What the hell, Durov."

"Do not feel you must thank me, *moy droog*. Consider it an early Christmas present."

Sir growled, "You know how I feel about those damn trees."

"I do and I felt the same, but…" Rytsar looked at Brie as she walked into the room with Hope. "I feel differently now."

"We have a perfectly acceptable one," Sir said, pointing to the bonsai.

Rytsar gave it a side glance. "Really?"

"If you need a tree so badly, why not put it in your own damn house?"

"I already have one, and it's bigger."

"Of course, it is." Sir shook his head, taking Hope from Brie's arms. "But I won't be pressured into ruining the aesthetics of the house or dealing with pine needles littering the floor."

"Isn't the smell divine?" Rytsar commented,

ignoring Sir's ire.

"I think so," Brie added meekly.

Sir smirked, shaking his head slowly as he stared at the tree.

Hope reached her hand out and Sir suddenly frowned, leaning forward as he looked into the boughs. "Is that the cat?"

"*Da*. Even the *kot* approves," Rytsar stated as if that was enough to convince him.

Hope's attention shifted to the lone ornament on the tree and she started babbling excitedly, grasping with her little fingers.

Sir obliged her and knelt so she could touch it. Hope tapped the ornament and giggled as it swung on the branch.

"Damn," he muttered to himself.

Rytsar looked over at Brie confidently.

Kneeling beside him, Brie pointed out the scene painted on the egg. "Look. It's my cabin in the snow."

Sir glanced up at Rytsar. "Clever."

He shrugged. "It was nothing, comrade. I wanted a part of Russia to be reflected on your tree. It's the least I could do."

"Spreading it on thick there, old friend."

Rytsar's voice suddenly became serious. "I

need this, brother."

Sir stood up and turned to face him. Brie saw the same haunted look in Rystar's eyes that she saw the first night of his return.

Sir nodded. "That is something I can understand and respect. For everything you've done for my family, I will accept this monstrosity of a tree with a full heart." Holding out his hand to Rytsar, he said, "As you seek to forget what you've experienced, I will seek to remember that there was a time when this holiday meant something to me." He glanced down at Hope cradled in his arms, an expression of fatherly concern on his face.

Shaking his hand solemnly, Rytsar agreed, pulling Sir in for a manly hug.

Brie was deeply touched by their exchange. Two strong men facing a holiday they had avoided for years, now choosing to experience the season through the wonder of Hope's eyes.

Brie glanced toward the tree to see Shadow had climbed down it and was stalking the ornament hanging on the limb. He rushed up to it, sat on his haunches, and gave it a light pat.

Hope broke out in giggles that made Brie smile. Her daughter started babbling to Shadow in earnest as if she was asking him to do it again.

The big black cat looked up at the baby and, keeping his gaze on Hope, patted the ornament again.

Hope burst out in strings of giggles that made all three of them laugh.

"So the tree stays, but it needs to go over there," Sir stated, pointing to the other side of the great room.

Rytsar nodded to his men, who proceeded with some difficulty, to transport the huge tree to Sir's preferred spot.

Looking at the immensity of it, Sir shook his head and muttered, "Babygirl, you've got a lot of decorations to buy."

Brie could hardly contain her excitement.

Although Brie hadn't said anything aloud, she was anxiously waiting for Hope to say her first word.

Having googled it, she knew that babies normally said their first word between six to twelve months. Because their little girl studied everyone so thoughtfully when they were talking, as well as the way she babbled endlessly to Shadow as if she were having a complicated conversation, Brie felt certain that Hope was close to uttering that highly anticipated first word.

But, the big question was—which word would she say?

On a lark, Master Anderson had mentioned to Brie that Hope's first word would be "Brad".

"It might sound like 'dad,'" he told her, "but she'll definitely be saying 'Brad.'"

Brie laughed, holding out her hand to him. "How much do you wanna bet, Master Anderson?"

He grinned. "Whoever loses has to do the other person's laundry…bare-chested."

With a twinkle in her eye, Brie told him, "I'll have to pass it by Sir, but I'll take you up on that bet. I would love to see you wash Hope's spit rags."

She could see Master Anderson gag a little before he took her hand and shook it.

Winning this bet was going to be all kinds of fun!

Naturally, Rytsar was certain his name would

be the first, especially since *"dyadya"* was an easy word to pronounce. He ribbed Sir hard about it.

"It is good that you insist on *moye solntse* calling you 'papa'. It eliminates any unnecessary arguments when she says my name first."

Sir chuckled. "I think you are in for a major disappointment, old friend. I come from a long line of Italians who've said 'papa' first. It's a family tradition." He looked at Brie and gave her an apologetic wink. "Sorry to disappoint you, babygirl."

She shrugged. "I know, I know...I've researched it and realize the chances of her saying 'mama' first are pretty slim, but I'm not giving up hope."

Hope let out a peal of laughter, thinking Brie had said her name.

Brie picked her up and touched noses with her. "You're too darn cute, sweet pea, and I know 'mama' is your favorite word because it's attached to me." She repeated the word, pronounced it more slowly. "Maa...maa..."

"Are you cheating, *radost moya*?" Rytsar accused.

"I'm just helping Hope expresses herself. Isn't that right, little girl?" She rubbed noses with Hope again before she set her on the ground.

Hope immediately crawled over to Shadow and reached out to touch him.

Sir looked at the cat with tenderness. "For an animal, he sure has a gentle way about him whenever he's with her."

"I have to admit, I was concerned at first," Rytsar admitted. "I remember when that *kot* tried to smother me at night with its body while I slept."

"I do remember that," Brie said laughing. "But I believe he thought you were the perfect body pillow."

Hope tried to grab Shadow's ear, but he kept flattening it to his head whenever she reached out to touch it. Hope seemed to think it was a game, and sat up so she could use both hands to grab his ears.

Shadow didn't move but he was uncanny with his timing, flattening his ears just as she was about to touch them and then raising them again as soon as she pulled her hands away.

It was a delightful source of entertainment for Hope.

"His patience is truly admirable," Brie said,

smiling down at the cat. "It's almost as if he understands she's only a child..."

They all heard it—a single syllable coming from Hope's lips—and the room became silent.

"What did you say, Hope?" Brie asked as she knelt on the floor, asking her to say it again.

"Doe."

Rytsar grinned. "You mean '*dya*' for '*dyadya*.'"

"Doe," Hope said again, smiling up at him.

Rytsar smacked Sir on the back. "*Dyadya* wins the day. What did I tell you, comrade?"

Sir chuckled. "I think you are being premature. She clearly said 'doe.'"

"What are you trying to tell us?" Brie asked her again, looking deep into Hope's dark brown eyes.

"Doe," she said, giggling as she reached out to touch Shadow.

Brie's jaw dropped. "I think she's saying Shadow's name."

Rytsar scoffed. "*Nyet*..."

Hope giggled again when the cat lowered his ears and cried enthusiastically, "Doe!"

Sir laughed. "Of all the important people in her life, she gives the honor to our cat."

"I can't believe it," Rytsar muttered. He

looked at Hope in earnest, asking, "Why, *moye solntse?* Why?"

Her big brown eyes twinkle in delight at her *dyadya* before she looked to the cat again. "Doe."

Rytsar smirked, accepting defeat. "*Da*. That is your Dow."

Brie picked up her phone and texted Master Anderson.

Guess who is going to be doing our laundry? Hope just said her first word.

A few seconds later, he texted back. **Damn. Hopefully she didn't say *dyadya* or I will never hear the end of it.**

Brie giggled as she typed.

Nope. But you'll never guess what it was!
I bet her first word was 'no'.
It rhymes with no. Hope said Dow.
Okay…
As in Shadow.
Oh, hell, no.

Brie laughed when she saw his response.

"What's so funny, babygirl?" Sir asked. He picked Hope up and said in a tender voice as he pointed at the cat, "Is that your Dow, little angel?"

"Dow," Hope agreed, grinning at the cat.

Brie giggled when she explained, "I texted

Master Anderson to let him know he lost the bet, and then I told him what her first word was. Let's just say, he's in shock."

Rytsar laughed, looking down at Shadow. "I guess I owe you a piece of bacon, *kot*."

New Insight

Ms. Clark was flying to LA for a short weekend trip. Don Castrillo, the famous BDSM photographer, had requested that she do a photo shoot. It made sense since the Domme was incredibly striking with her long blonde hair, voluptuous body, and those seductive red lips. They also had a personal connection because he had scened with her at the Haven a few years ago.

Hearing that Ms. Clark was going to be in town, Sir offered to let his longtime friend stay at the beach house. Brie was shocked when the Domme actually said yes. She was a fiercely independent woman and didn't seem the type to have the patience for a baby in her midst.

Sir reassured Brie before he went to pick the

Domme up at the airport. "I know Samantha can be a challenge at times, but I feel this is important, babygirl."

She trusted Sir without question, but as she readied the guest bedroom, Brie felt her nerves kick in. Ms. Clark was intense, and there had always been a strange vibe between Brie and the Domme.

During Brie's six-week course at the Submissive Training Center, Ms. Clark had been overly strict with her and critical as a trainer, and she was openly displeased when Sir collared Brie on graduation day.

Eventually, the Domme had come to accept that Brie was a permanent part of Sir's life, but an uneasiness still remained between them.

Brie suspected it had something to do with Rytsar.

Ms. Clark had a complicated past with the Russian, and Brie had only knew the barest of details about what had happened between them. However, she was certain it didn't help that Rytsar had chosen Brie at her first auction and had remained close to her to this day.

Following the dangerous rescue in Russia, Rytsar had forgiven Samantha for her wrongs against him. Still, there remained a level of tension between the two Dominants, and that had seemingly been transferred to Brie.

Despite it, Brie was determined to make the Domme feel comfortable while she visited their home. She wanted to honor Sir's long-standing relationship with the Domme.

After readying the room, Brie waited nervously by the door until she heard Sir's Lotus Evora pull up.

She opened it to greet them and was struck again by how beautiful Ms. Clark looked in her formfitting business suit and sexy stilettos.

"Mrs. Davis," she said curtly as she walked past Brie and into the house.

The moment that Ms. Clark saw the giant tree, she turned on Sir. "What's happened to you?"

He chuckled. "One word—Durov."

She looked back at the tree. "And here I thought it was Brie who had made you soft."

Sir glanced at Brie with a look of pride. "Brianna and I challenge each other in every aspect of our lives, but we also respect each other's boundaries."

He took Brie's hand and kissed it in front of

Ms. Clark, looking into Brie's eyes as he did so. Brie could hear his voice in her head saying, *I am well pleased,* and it made her heart swell with pride.

Ms. Clark tsked. "Well, it's obvious that Durov doesn't respect boundaries."

"Actually, we have an understanding between us, so I agreed to the tree." Sir glanced at the tall pine tree decorated in blue and gold with accents of red. "Hasn't Brie done a beautiful job of decorating it?"

Ms. Clark stared hard at him. "Thane, I'm struggling to accept this unexpected change in you."

His smile was easy when he answered, "If you aren't constantly growing, then you are stagnant."

"Are you trying to insinuate that I'm stagnant?"

Sir chose not to answer her question directly. "Samantha, you told me how shocked you were by how I've changed, and I've simply answered you."

But it was obvious Ms. Clark thought otherwise as she glanced back at the tree and stared at it with a far-off look, as she digested his words.

After several moments, she stated matter-of-factly, "It's a nice tree, Brianna."

Brie looked at Ms. Clark in surprise, shocked that the Domme had given her a compliment. She gave Sir a questioning glance and saw that he was quietly observing Ms. Clark.

Brie could read the concern on his face and wondered what he was thinking.

Ms. Clark let out a drawn-out sigh and turned away from the Christmas tree. "So, where's the baby?"

"She's down for her nap," Brie explained. "Would you like me to get her?"

"Don't disturb the child. I was simply curious."

Ms. Clark turned to Sir. "It must be difficult to be a father and still remain true to your calling."

"It is a challenge, yes. But you know I've always enjoyed challenges."

She let out a sharp laugh. "Well, you certainly proved that by remaining friends with me all these years."

Sir met her gaze and said in a serious tone, "I never abandon my friends."

Ms. Clark actually teared up, which floored

Brie.

"No, you've always been there for me, Thane."

She had never seen the Domme in such a vulnerable state before. It was unnerving.

The doorbell rang, interrupting their conversation.

Brie went to answer it, explaining to Sir that she was expecting a package. When she saw the box on the porch, she cried, "It came!"

"What is it, babygirl?"

Brie smiled at him as she hugged the box to her. "My mom sent their Nativity set to us. She and I used to set it up every year when I was a little girl." Brie smiled as she looked at the box. "It's one of my favorite memories of Christmas. My mom told me she wants Hope to have the same memories growing up."

"That was very thoughtful of her," Sir replied.

But Ms. Clark snorted. "First a tree? Now a Nativity set? You are becoming completely vanilla before my very eyes."

"It has nothing to do with becoming vanilla," he corrected her. "I want to fill my daughter's life with traditions that she can look back on and hold onto as an adult—just as my father did for me."

Ms. Clark shrugged. "I wish my childhood memories brought comfort, but they're all connected to my brother, Joseph, and it hurts too much."

She now had Brie's full attention. This was the first she'd ever heard that Ms. Clark had a brother.

"That surprises me, Samantha, because you don't avoid me even though I closely resemble him."

Sir looks like her brother?

Brie did her best to remain calm, but she was rocked by that shocking revelation.

Ms. Clark looked at him, stating hesitantly, "You insisted I separate the two of you, and I have fought every day to do that."

"So, it's still a struggle for you even after all these years?" Sir asked, sounding surprised.

Ms. Clark suddenly looked uncomfortable. "I never told you because…I knew it would upset you, Thane." She looked at him in earnest. "I couldn't bear it if you cut me out of your life. It would be too much after everything that's happened."

Sir cleared his throat. "Honestly, I'm shocked, Samantha."

The fearful look Ms. Clark gave Sir made it obvious that she regretted having said anything.

"I understand grief never ends after losing someone you love deeply," he stated in an even tone. "You and I both know that, but for it to still be so fresh for you deeply troubles me."

"What are you saying, Thane?" she whimpered.

Sir's look of concern turned into one of compassion when he saw the fear in her eyes. "After all these years, do you really think I would abandon you now, Samantha?"

"But you were adamant that I never think of Joseph when I'm around you. And still, it's impossible for me." Brie noticed her hands were shaking when she said, "I wouldn't survive if I lost you, too."

Ms. Clark's voice sounded so broken that Brie felt a wave of compassion for her.

In that moment, Brie suddenly understood how traumatic it must have been for Ms. Clark the day Sir's plane crashed. Brie vividly remembered the beautiful bouquet that the Domme had sent to her when Sir was fighting for his life.

Ms. Clark must have been crazy with fear that he would die, but she had kept her distance out of respect for Rytsar, whom she assumed was watching over Sir at the time.

Seeing the Domme like this, Brie felt sympathy for her. All these years, Ms. Clark had been secretly mourning the loss of her brother. The way she treated Sir had always confused Brie. She'd always acted more like a fiercely protective sister than a friend to Sir.

It all made sense now.

But Brie would never have guessed that Sir had essentially become Joseph's replacement in Ms. Clark's life.

"Samantha, I wish you had spoken to me about this sooner," Sir stated.

Ms. Clark shook her head. "It wasn't worth the risk to me."

"So instead, you've suffered needlessly all these years, holding onto his ghost rather than moving forward?"

"I couldn't face losing your friendship on top of everything else I've lost. Can't you understand that, Thane?"

"What I understand is that you've kept your grief buried for so long, you will need a therapist to unravel all the emotions you've repressed. You've run away long enough and I'm afraid that my presence in your life is at the root of the issue."

Ms. Clark's eyes widened in fear. "No! I wouldn't be here without you. Don't you dare leave me now." Her voice broke with emotion, and it seemed to Brie that she was on the verge of breaking down.

Sir put his hand on her shoulder. "I'm not going anywhere. Brie and I will act as your support through the process, but you must promise to seek professional help. It is no longer a choice, Samantha. It's obvious you are incapable of moving past this on your own."

Ms. Clark crossed her arms and stared at him in defiance.

Sir gazed into her eyes and said, "I know it doesn't seem possible now, but there will come a time when you can think back on your brother and smile."

Ms. Clark shook her head violently, the tears returning to her eyes. "Never…"

Putting his hands on both of her shoulders, he stated firmly, "Yes, you will. I saw my father shoot himself in the head. While that memory will never leave me, I have many others that I choose to embrace. It makes it possible to remember him with a sense of joy."

She stared at Sir, looking as if she desperately wanted to believe him.

"Trust me."

Ms. Clark fiddled with a button on her dress. "You're not angry with me for hiding this from you all these years?"

Her voice reminded Brie of an anxious child.

"Angry? No." Sir's expression softened. "However, I am disheartened to learn you've wasted so many years suffering in silence." He glanced at Brie. "But maybe, like me, you needed someone to push you in the right direction."

Ms. Clark turned to face Brie, her expression ripe with emotion. "You've had a greater influence over him than I thought."

Brie met Ms. Clark's intense gaze and said simply, "I love him."

Pain flashed in the Domme's eyes, but she nodded to Brie before turning away.

A Confession

Later that evening, while Sir was off meeting with a client, Brie opened the box her mother had sent. Inside, was a decorative green box marked with her mother's beautiful handwriting:

Bennett Family Nativity

Just seeing the old box made Brie's heart burst with happiness. Even though she didn't consider herself a religious person, Brie had always loved the story of the Nativity.

Looking at Hope, Brie said with a smile, "This is a special tradition my mommy shared with me when I was a little girl." Reaching out, she playfully tweaked her daughter's small toes. "And now I am going to share it with you, sweet pea."

Brie lifted the lid and breathed a sigh of joy when she saw the carefully wrapped pieces that made up the set.

She heard Ms. Clark emerge from the guest bedroom and watched her walk toward the kitchen. When she saw Brie with the lid in her hands she asked, "Do you mind if I watch?"

Normally, Brie would have balked at the request, but after today's conversation, she felt differently toward Ms. Clark. She no longer felt as intimidated by her.

"Sure."

Ms. Clark walked over to the couch to join them.

Brie was kneeling on the floor next to the coffee table. Using the bonsai tree as a backdrop for the simple Nativity scene, Brie took out the three wooden pieces that made up the stable and joined them together, setting it on the table as she explained to Hope, "Mary was ready to give birth and Joseph…" As soon as she said the name, Brie stopped and glanced nervously at Ms. Clark. She realized it might be upsetting for her.

"Go on," Ms. Clark insisted, showing no emotion.

Looking back at Hope, Brie continued hesitantly. "All of the inns in Bethlehem were full…but there was one innkeeper who gave the couple permission to use his stable for the night."

Brie reached into the box and picked up the star. She carefully unwrapped it while she said, "That night, Mary gave birth to her son, Jesus, under a star that had appeared in the sky."

She hung it on the bonsai tree. Taking the tiny wooden manger out of the box, Brie placed it inside the stable. "There was no crib, so they put the baby in a manger full of straw.

Brie unwrapped each of the wise men dressed in their silks and finery, as well as their camels which were laden with gifts. She showed each one to Hope before placing them on the table. "From the east, three wise men came to see the newborn, bearing gifts of gold, frankincense, and myrrh."

Brie especially enjoyed unwrapping the shepherds. She loved their scraggly beards, simple clothing, and the look of reverence on their faces. "The shepherds in the east also came to honor the baby."

With reverence, Brie unwrapped the couple

and placed them at the head of the manger. "Joseph and Mary stood next to the manger, proudly watching over their newborn son."

She then reached into the box, pulling out the individual animals, explaining, "The animals in the stable felt protective of the baby and lay near him." She smiled as she set the cow and the donkey on either side of the manger and then placed the tiny lamb near Mary.

"Then an angel came down from Heaven and declared, 'Glory to God in the highest, and on Earth, peace and goodwill toward men.'" Unwrapping the angel with her wings outspread, Brie placed her behind Joseph and Mary.

"And this is the little baby who gave hope to the world," Brie told her, showing her daughter the beautifully painted child.

Brie laid the child in the manger and explained to her daughter, "Every Christmas, we celebrate the birth of Jesus who embraces all who seek forgiveness in His name."

Ms. Clark had remained silent until the end. Brie held her breath when the Domme opened her mouth to speak. She fully expected her to say something derogatory.

Instead, she said in an almost wistful voice,

"Although I don't believe in all that religious crap, there is something alluring about the idea of a person being washed free of their sins."

Brie nodded, surprised to hear Ms. Clark speaking so personally.

She met Brie's gaze when she said with remorse, "What I wouldn't do to take back what happened that night…"

Her eyes were drowning in sadness, making Brie's heart ache for her.

"All I wanted to do was get him safely to bed."

Brie had thought she was talking about Joseph until Ms. Clark said, "But Rytsar insisted that I stay and come to his bed. How could I deny him?"

A cold chill went down Brie's spine when she realized Ms. Clark was speaking about the night she had violated Rytsar.

"….I'd never felt such red-hot chemistry with a person, and I have never experienced it since."

Brie's heart started racing, unsure this was something she wanted to know.

Ms. Clark stared at Brie, admitting, "Rytsar is a force of nature. It was true then as much as it is now. So, when he asked me to his bed, I went."

The intensity of her gaze, along with the tone of her voice let Brie know she was speaking to her as an equal—two women who had both experienced the power of the man—and not a Dominant talking to a sub.

"We were rough with each other...we always were, each of us wanting control of the other...but that's when I made the fatal error. I needed a shot of liquid courage to do what I wanted. When I discovered Rytsar had Patron hidden away, I took a shot, and then another."

Ms. Clark looked down at the floor, the memory obviously causing her great pain. "My family has a long history of alcoholism, and that particular tequila makes me crazy. All the boys I had before thought it was cute how wild I would get when I drank the stuff, and I wanted to be irresistible to Rytsar that night. I needed him to want me more than any other woman he'd ever known.

She paused for a moment. "But...I didn't understand the great harm I was capable of."

Goosebumps rose on Brie's skin.

"Rytsar had me take the role of submissive

on several occasions prior to that night, and each time I learned something new about myself."

She looked at Brie sadly. "I wanted to give that gift to him…"

Brie shook her head, knowing Rytsar was incapable of submitting to anyone.

Ms. Clark told her, "I truly believed I was the Dominant he needed to make that happen. I had planned it all out in my head before, so when the opportunity presented itself, I was too turned on and drunk on Patron to control myself. I craved the idea of having the great Rytsar Durov submit to me."

She closed her eyes. "I took his commands to stop as simply his Russian stubbornness. I was certain that once I'd broken down his resistance, I would have him eating out of my hand. I was so sure of it. I even used his cat o' nines, wanting him to know the power behind his instrument. But…"

She opened her eyes, tears streaming down her face. "I didn't know what I was doing and I hurt him…I hurt him so badly." The look in her eyes was one of horror. "It was like I suddenly came out of a stupor after I saw the damage I had done."

Her lips began trembling. "I couldn't face it. So, instead of helping him, I ran, hoping against hope that it was a bad dream and I would wake up from it."

She swallowed several times, struggling to regain her voice. "I didn't believe it was real until Thane came to check on me. One look at his face and I knew…"

She let out a ragged sigh. "I had to face my own brutality and it was terrifying."

Ms. Clark sat there in silence, seeming to relive that moment as Brie watched.

She shook her head slowly, a look of devastation on her face. "I murdered our relationship that night. I knew it in my heart, but I wasn't willing to face that I'd killed what we had. I tried everything to win back Rytsar's trust, but there was no going back."

She met Brie's gaze again. "Do you know what that's like?"

When Brie didn't answer, she shrugged, stating dismissively. "Of course you wouldn't. You're Little Brie Perfect."

Her derogatory nickname irritated Brie, but she chose to ignore it. It was clear that the anger Ms. Clark was aiming at her was actually directed at herself.

Brie replied in a soft but somber tone, "You must be relieved that Rytsar finally forgave you. He is not a man to do that easily."

"I am...but it hasn't actually changed anything. What I did sixteen years ago cannot be washed away. It will always stand between us." She glanced at the Nativity. "That's why some fairy tale about sins being taken from a person is compelling to me. To face a new day without the burden of what I've done would be freeing on a level you can't understand."

Brie was suddenly struck by a thought. "Have you ever talked to Marquis Gray about this? He might be able to help."

Ms. Clark huffed. "I haven't opened up to another person besides Thane about what happened until tonight. I am not about to bare my soul to that man."

"I believe he can help you," Brie gently offered.

Ms. Clark pursed her lips, saying nothing.

"Since you've been so open with me, I think you should know this. Even though you hurt Rytsar all those years ago, you saved his life in Russia when no one else could." Tears came to

Brie's eyes when she confessed, "I will be forever grateful to you for that."

The Domme met Brie's gaze. "I could never have lived with myself if I hadn't."

Brie nodded, believing her.

"So," Ms. Clark huffed. "There is no reason for you to be grateful to me."

"But I am," Brie insisted, picking up Hope, who had fallen asleep during their conversation. Cradling her daughter against her, Brie kissed the top of Hope's head.

"Thank you for indulging me this evening, Mrs. Davis," Ms. Clark stated in a formal voice.

Brie understood by her tone that they had returned to their normal dynamic. However, she now had personal insight into the Domme that she'd never had before, and it made the woman's abrasive demeanor easier to accept.

Brie was uncertain about what impact it might have moving forward, but tonight's conversation had changed her feelings toward Ms. Clark forever.

Ghost from the Past

When Mary asked Brie to meet at a coffee shop, she knew something was up.

Instead of the heart-to-heart Brie was hoping for, Mary invited her to a holiday party being held in downtown LA for all the top Hollywood bigwigs in the film industry.

"Stinks, you need to get out so important people in the industry start putting a face to your name. Besides, I'm so fucking sick of these people. I need you as a distraction."

Brie snorted, taking a sip of her latte. "Is that the real reason you want me to go?"

Mary pursed her lips and rolled her eyes. "Of course not. I'm planning my second line of defense if Greg gives you any shit about your film."

Brie appreciated having Mary on her side. The girl was exceptionally smart, even if she was a salty bitch.

"I'll ask Sir if the date works for him."

"It's best if you didn't."

Brie frowned. "Why?"

"Greg is iffy about Sir Davis. He gets that way around any strong Dominant. I think he needs to feel like he's the top dog in the room."

Brie could totally imagine that, having worked with Greg Holloway in the past. The man wanted things his way or no way. It was going to make working with him to complete and release the newest documentary extremely challenging. Even though she was a submissive, when it came to this film, she could already feel her alpha side coming out.

"How should I dress for the party?"

"To the hilt, girl. This one is a big deal."

"Well, that should be fun. I always like an excuse to get dolled up."

Mary leaned in, telling her, "I highly recommend getting your hair and makeup done professionally. You need to look flawless."

"You're making it sound more like a job interview."

"It is, Stinks."

Brie frowned, taking another sip of her latte. "Well, that doesn't sound like any fun at all."

"It won't be, but that's not why you're going. Remember that."

Brie asked Sir to pick out her dress, trusting in his tastes for the important event. Although he disliked the fact that he wasn't invited, Sir agreed with Mary that it was important for Brie to attend.

"Be charming and confident, but make them exceedingly aware that you are a gifted director, not just another pretty face."

"I will, Sir."

He helped her into the dress he had chosen, careful not to mess up her hair or makeup. The formfitting dress was a crimson full-length gown with long sleeves. It fully covered her front but had a low draping back.

Conservative but elegant.

Putting his arms around her as they both gazed into the mirror, Sir said, "I don't want them staring at your breasts while you talk." He kissed her lightly on the neck. "I want them to know you are not only fully woman, but intelligent, talented, and fiercely determined."

Brie smiled, gazing at Sir's reflection. "I love you, Sir."

He stared back at her with admiration. "My goddess."

When Brie left for the party, she felt ready to take on the world. Sir insisted she take his Lotus, which made her feel like a total badass when she pulled up and gave the valet the keys.

She headed up the elevator, feeling strangely calm but excited about the night ahead. With a confidence born of drive, passion, and the strength of Sir's love, she walked into the party and surveyed the crowd.

Mary immediately sauntered up to her. "Well, shit, Stinks. You clean up nice."

Brie played with Sir's collar around her neck. "You told me to dress for success."

"Well, you'll definitely be turning heads in that dress," Mary said. She suddenly grabbed Brie's hand. "And your red nails match your lipstick perfectly."

"I took inspiration from Ms. Clark."

Mary nodded in approval. "I have a good feeling about tonight."

"Me, too," Brie agreed, thrilled to be in a room with such important people.

Instead of nerves, Brie was charged with purpose. Not only was she about to show Greg Holloway how serious she was, but everyone in attendance would soon know the depth of passion she felt for her newest film.

Mary started making the rounds, introducing her to the people she felt Brie needed to meet.

Brie felt like a natural, handling each conversation with ease as she steered the discussion toward her documentary. She was pleased to learn that many of them were familiar with her first film.

To Mary's credit, she stuck by Brie's side, eliminating any bystanders who tried to join the conversation, wanting to redirect the focus on themselves.

Two hours into it, Mary declared it was time for a break. Heading to the private bar, she asked Brie what she wanted to drink.

"What do they have?"

"All the traditional stuff plus some holiday specialty drinks."

Hope's First Christmas

"Those sound like fun."

Mary looked at the list at the bar. "Looks like they have Fireside Glogg, Naughty Nog, Peppermint Punch, and Santa's Kiss.

"Oh, I'll take Santa's Kiss."

"You got it."

While they waited for their drinks, Brie observed a group of women snorting coke at a coffee table.

"It's a staple at these things," Mary explained nonchalantly. "Everyone in Hollywood is always looking for the next buzz." Mary turned away from them and took the drinks the bartender handed her.

Brie looked around the room at all the people with their fake smiles and laughter and said, "You'd think BDSM would be enough of a high."

Mary laughed, handing Brie her drink. "Any here are just wannabes. I told you. Greg doesn't like competition."

Directing Brie to a table laden with expensive hors d'oeuvres, Mary grabbed a plate and started loading it up.

Brie took her own plate, excited to try a bite of everything on the table.

When Mary saw what foods she was taking, she stopped Brie. "Keep it simple, Stinks. Shrimp and raw vegetables. Easy finger food. We're not here to eat. We're here to socialize."

"But it all looks so delicious."

"You need to look classy at all times, and you definitely don't want to be caught with something in your teeth when you're talking to these people."

"Heard," Brie answered, reluctantly dumping the spinach quiche and caviar from her plate.

Mary directed her to a quiet area and asked, "So what do you think of the evening so far?"

Brie scanned the room. "I'm enjoying myself, actually. There's certainly a lot of influential people here. I can't thank you enough for all the introductions."

"You're seriously killing it, and we're not done yet." Mary nodded to an unassuming young man wearing a black cap with the words "I'm not okay".

"I like the hat," Brie said, chuckling.

"He's our next target. Finn Jamison may not look like much, but the last two films he produced were blockbusters. He's definitely someone you want to know."

Brie took a sip of her Santa's Kiss out of the martini glass rimmed with fine sugar and purred, "Yum! Raspberry and lemon with a kiss of coconut and something else I can't quite put my finger on…"

"Stop analyzing your damn drink and suck it down, woman," Mary ordered. Downing her own, Mary ate one more shrimp before handing her plate and glass over to a server passing by.

Brie rolled her eyes. "You're such a slave driver."

"I'm not the one who needs to meet these people."

Taking the hint, Brie quickly finished her drink, popping a carrot into her mouth.

Before they could make their way to Finn, however, Greg Holloway showed up. Slipping an arm around Mary in a possessive manner, he said to Brie, "I see you've hijacked my arm candy this evening."

"Mary's been kind enough to keep me company," Brie answered lightly even though his presence instantly caused her defenses to go up.

Holloway looked her up and down. "I find it hard to believe that you are the same Brie Bennett I worked with a few years ago."

Brie lifted her chin slightly. "I'm not. As you know, I'm married now and my name is Mrs. Davis."

"Heh…" He chuckled, pressing Mary against him. "So, tell me, is that Master of yours doing a good job of keeping you in line?"

Brie found his comment offensive and was about to correct him when Mary bumped her hip against the man in a playful manner. "Hey, Tiger, Rodney was asking for you. He didn't happen to catch you by any chance?"

"No." Holloway's brow furrowed as he scanned the room. He let go of Mary, muttering, "I'd better find that little shit and see what the hell went wrong now…"

After he left, Mary smiled slyly. "Lucky for me, he's an easy man to distract."

Brie wanted to talk more about him, but Mary grabbed Brie's arm. "Now's our chance."

The two walked up to Finn, who lit up the instant he saw Mary. "Hey, good looking. Where's the boss man?"

"Greg's chasing Rodney down."

"Poor Rodney."

Mary gave him a charming smile before turning to Brie. "Finn, I'd like to introduce you to

Brie Davis. She's got a documentary about BDSM, which I happen to star in. She's looking to get it released."

Brie found Finn easy to talk to and down to Earth, making for an interesting conversation. Everything seemed to be going well until she caught sight of someone out of the corner of her eye as he walked past.

The instant Brie saw Darius, her heart stopped and she felt the blood drain from her face.

"What's wrong, Brie?" Mary whispered.

Brie's stomach twisted into knots, and she suddenly felt like she was going to throw up.

Mary grabbed her arm and asked Finn to excuse them as she raced Brie to the bathroom. Once inside, she locked the door and asked, "Are you all right?"

Brie barely made it to the toilet before she heaved.

"What happened out there?" Mary demanded with concern.

After Brie finished heaving up her drink, she got to her feet slowly, feeling as if she was having an out-of-body experience as she washed her hands and mouth. "There is someone here who assaulted me when I was young."

"Who the hell is he? I'll fucking kick his ass."

Brie stood there, staring at her reflection in the mirror while all those terrible feelings came rushing back. She relived the horror of that moment when Darius forced her to the ground and choked her senseless while he kissed her and groped her young breasts.

Mary turned her around and hugged her, holding her tight.

Her open compassion broke the dam of emotions inside Brie, and she started to cry.

Mary growled. "I'm about to go apeshit all over somebody's ass in a second. Just tell me what he looks like."

As much as she wanted to take Mary up on the offer, Brie knew what she needed to do.

Building up her courage, Brie slowly wiped away her tears and fixed her makeup. Straightening her back, she took a deep breath before unlocking the door and opening it.

"Darius doesn't get to control me anymore."

With her head held high, Brie walked out the door. She wasn't sure what she would say once she found him, but she needed to confront the man who had haunted her nightmares for years.

However, Brie felt both dismay and relief when someone informed Mary that Darius had left with a large group of people just minutes before.

"What do you want to do, Stinks?" Mary asked her.

"I want to go home."

"You got it. I'll beat the shit out of that motherfucker another day."

Brie smiled, knowing that Mary really would if she asked.

As she was leaving, Finn Jamison came up and stopped her. "Hey, Brie, I'd like to talk to you again." Handing her his business card, he said, "Give me a ring and we'll set something up."

Brie smiled and thanked Finn. "I look forward to it."

Mary walked her out and waited beside her as the valet went to get her car. "I'd be happy to drive you home, if you want."

"I'll be fine," Brie said.

After a brief pause, Mary told her, "If you ever want to talk, day or night, you've got my number."

"I appreciate that." Smiling sadly, Brie turned

to her and added, "I really did enjoy tonight."

"I did, too, Stinks. You absolutely killed it by scoring the biggest coup of them all. Getting Finn's number is a major victory."

As the car pulled up, Brie told her, "Tonight was about the film. Darius doesn't get to steal that away from me."

"No, he doesn't," Mary agreed. "And I think you just became my new hero."

As Brie drove home, she made a New Year's resolution to herself. Rather than live her life dreading the day she might run into Darius again, she would seek him out and confront the man—on her own terms.

Christmas Kittens

Brie got an exciting text from Master Anderson the following week.

They're here, and I must say they're darn cute.
The kittens?
Yes. She had two.
Oh my goodness, can I come over to see them? I insist!

Brie walked into Sir's office. "Cayenne just had her babies, Sir."

Sir glanced up from his computer. "Don't tell me. He wants you to rush over to see them?"

"Master Anderson insisted."

He chuckled. "I find it strange that my friend can have such paternal feelings toward his cats, but he openly dislikes babies."

"I think it's a case of self-denial, Sir. We both

know he would be over the moon if he ever became a father."

Sir snorted. "After seeing how he is with the cats, he's certain to be completely obnoxious about it."

Brie smiled. "But, he'd be adorable."

"Let me finish up here and I'll join you. Tell him we'll both see him in a few hours."

"Oh, my goodness. I can't wait! Shey is going to be so surprised when she finds out."

Sir looked back at his screen, chuckling. "Funny what a man will do for love."

Brie looked over at Shadow and smiled, remembering when Master Anderson called her two months ago with his shocking proposal.

"Young Brie, I have a confession to make."

She giggled into the phone. "What, Master Anderson?"

"I never had Cayenne spayed."

Her jaw literally dropped. "What? You do you realize she could get pregnant by one of her own kittens?"

"There's no worry about that. I had them all fixed as soon as they were old enough."

"Why didn't you spay Cayenne, too?"

"Uh…" He laughed uncomfortably. "She's such a good mother. I didn't want to take that away from her."

Brie shook her head, grinning. "Well, Cayenne must be in heat a lot."

"She is. In fact, she's in heat right now and it's driving me nuts."

Brie laughed. "You have only yourself to blame."

"I know, I know. But, it got me thinking. Shey is leaving to take care of her mother in a few weeks."

"Is something wrong?" Brie asked in concern.

"No, but her mother is having a double knee replacement and will be completely incapacitated for several weeks. Afterward, she will still need help with rehabilitation until she can take care of herself and her household again."

"It's wonderful Shey can be there for her mom, but that must be hard to be separated for so long."

"Shey is dreading being away for such an extended amount of time, and is especially unhappy that we are going to miss Christmas together. So, I thought, what better way to bring a smile to her face every day she's gone than a cute baby kitten."

"Are you serious?"

"Completely. I'll surprise her on Christmas morning with a video and take the kitten to her myself once it's weaned."

"What are you going to do with the other kittens?"

He shrugged. "I'm certain I can find homes for them."

"You aren't planning to keep them too, are you, Master Anderson?" she teased.

He chuckled. "Heck no. My hands are full enough as it is. But if you're in the market for a tiny addition, I'll be happy to share the love."

Brie giggled. "I definitely don't see Sir adopting another animal anytime soon."

"His loss. So, you'll swing by then?"

She giggled, excited at the prospect of Shadow and Cayenne mating again. "You are about to make two cats very happy."

"Let's not even go there."

"When do you want me to bring Shadow

over?"

"The sooner the better. Cayenne is desperate." Brie could hear the cat's trilling meows in the background.

On the drive over, Brie kept smiling at Shadow. "All your patience has finally paid off, proud papa. You are about to meet up with your beautiful woman again, and I've been told she's been missing you something fierce."

When Brie arrived at the house, Shadow instantly perked up as if he could already smell that Cayenne was in heat.

The cat stared at the door intently as she walked up to his house. Master Anderson opened it before she even had a chance to ring the doorbell.

The bullwhip master stared at Shadow, his eyes narrowing with distrust. The cat's gaze was equally intense as he twitched his tail back and forth.

"I can't believe I'm really doing this..." Master Anderson muttered to Brie.

Cayenne's desperate meow came from somewhere inside the house and Shadow instantly responded, squirming in Brie's arms, wanting to join her.

"Looks like love is in the air," Brie exclaimed happily.

He grimaced. "That's one way to put it."

Master Anderson led Brie to the room he had designated for their reunion. The moment he opened the door, Shadow leaped out of Brie's arms and headed straight to Cayenne.

She ran to him, the two touching noses before she meowed, prostrating herself on the floor and rolling her hips side to side.

"Way more than I need to see," Master Anderson stated, shutting the door hurriedly. "Let's go out back before I completely lose it."

He headed to the back door and escorted Brie out, shutting the door. "I cannot begin to explain how difficult this is for me."

Brie grinned at him. "It's a part of nature."

Master Anderson groaned. "It is a hard thing to accept when she's your own."

"Said every father in the world."

"I suppose," he said, laughing. "If those two didn't make such cute kittens, I wouldn't be able to handle what that black bastard is doing to my Cayenne right now."

She found it amusing that he felt that way. "Really, it's no different than any sub who submits to your bullwhip. They willingly accept the pain because it brings them pleasure."

He grunted. "So, you are comparing me to the cat now?"

"Yes. You are both gentlemen who take care of their women."

Master Anderson huffed, looking at the door worriedly.

"And, since you've invited Shadow to mate with her, you're going to have to start calling him by his given name. 'Black bastard' is no longer an option."

He gave Brie a chagrined look and stared at his watch. "Do you think it's been long enough?"

"I'm sure. Cats are pretty quick."

Master Anderson headed back in.

"Could Shadow see his children before we leave?" Brie asked as she followed behind him.

Master Anderson chuckled. "I suppose he's entitled to it."

Brie opened the door and found Cayenne licking Shadow.

"See, Master Anderson? She loves him."

He frowned. "I suppose it's possible."

But the moment Cayenne started to make

that trilling meow again and flattened herself to the floor, Master Anderson barked, "Why don't you take him to see his kids? Pronto!"

Brie picked up the huge black cat who let out a mournful meow as she carried him out of the room. Master Anderson quickly shut the door behind her.

"I know you're sad, Shadow," Brie told that cat, "but we have a wonderful surprise for you."

Master Anderson opened the door to the old guest bedroom, which he'd transformed into a cat sanctuary. It had an attached, screened-in pen with cat ramps, cat cubbies, and multiple scratching posts outside with an entrance through a plastic flap in the window.

As soon as Brie set Shadow on the floor, the calico ran up to greet him. The big black Tomcat started purring loudly.

"They've missed each other," Brie exclaimed joyfully.

Master Anderson looked down at the little calico with tenderness. "I ended up calling this one Paprika."

"Oh, that's an adorable name for her," Brie cooed. "Tell me all their names."

He pointed to a slim black cat that was approaching Shadow. "That there is Chipotle. He's got a real sense of humor. And that cute little orange tabby sitting on the window ledge is Nutmeg. She's a shy little thing."

"Peppercorn is heading in right now. He's all kinds of curious," Master Anderson said proudly as Brie watched the black cat push his way through the plastic flap. As soon as he spotted Shadow, the cat jumped down and ran to him.

Master Anderson walked over to the window and lifted the flap up. "Hey, Ghost Pepper and Saffron, your 'daddy' has come for a visit."

Brie peeked out to see the other female tabby and a large black cat who looked a lot like Shadow except for his blue eyes.

"So, he's Ghost Pepper, huh?"

"I call him Ghost for short."

When the big cat entered the window, Brie called out. "Hey, Ghost! I can't believe how much you've grown since I saw you last."

He glanced in Brie's direction and jumped down, heading toward her. He rubbed his cheek against her leg, purring loudly.

"Consider yourself claimed," Anderson chuckled.

"You don't have any issues with Ghost even

though he looks so much like his father?"

He looked down at the black cat fondly. "Nah, Ghost and I are best buds. He likes watching me practice the bullwhip. The others run away when I start cracking the whip due to the harsh sound, but he seems fascinated by the bullwhip."

"How interesting…"

Brie wondered if Ghost had inherited Shadow's intelligence as well as his looks, as she watched him slowly stroll over to greet his father.

"Funny thing. I recently went through my closet in this room and you'll never guess what I came across."

She smiled. "I haven't a clue."

Master Anderson opened the closet door and pulled something out of a suit jacket hanging there. "You wouldn't have any idea where this might have come from?"

Brie squeaked when she saw it. "Oh my goodness!" It was one of the whoopee cushions.

"How many did you end up hiding in my house that night? I still come across them in the oddest places."

She burst out in giggles. "I think Rytsar

bought like fifty."

Master Anderson shook his head. "Such an odd man…"

"Were you surprised?" Brie asked, grinning.

"Hell, yeah, but I never understood why there were six of them in my washing machine."

Brie blushed. "You came home too soon. I didn't know where else to put them."

Master Anderson laughed. "So, I caught you red-handed but I just didn't know it."

"Yes! Did you like our little prank?"

"Oh, it was special, darlin'. Especially the night Shey came over and sat on the couch opposite of the one I normally use. You should have seen her red face when that whoopee let loose."

"Poor Shey!" Brie giggled.

"Naturally, she was embarrassed and thought I had set it out for her. It wasn't until I showed her the massive amount of whoopee cushions I had collected around the house that she finally believed I wasn't the culprit."

"Sorry about that, Master Anderson. Why didn't you ever confront us about it?"

He smiled charmingly. "Do you know the best way to get back at a prankster?"

She shook her head.

"You pretend nothing happened and they can't ask you about it without outing themselves—that gives you the final laugh."

"You are an evil genius."

"I am the master of practical jokes. Never forget that, young Brie," he said with a wink.

Brie and Sir, along with Hope and Shadow, headed over to see the new kittens as soon as Sir finished for the night.

"This is so exciting," Brie exclaimed.

Sir smiled, keeping his eyes on the road. "I can't believe my friend is now the owner of nine cats."

"Oh, he's planning to give them away," she assured him.

"He's giving one to Shey, who practically lives at his house as it is. Do you really see him giving up the other kitten?"

"No, Sir, actually I can't," she laughed.

When they arrived, Brie exclaimed with joy. "Oh, look, Hope, Master Anderson's house is all lit up for Christmas."

"I can guarantee you that Shey had something to do with that," Sir said, taking Hope out of her car seat.

Brie walked up Master Anderson's walkway with Shadow in her arms, thoroughly charmed by all the twinkling Christmas lights. "It reminds me of my old neighborhood."

When Sir pressed the doorbell, "Jingle Bells" started to play.

"Oh, Lord," Sir muttered under his breath.

"That's adorable," Brie giggled.

Master Anderson answered the door with a huge grin on his face. "Are you ready to meet my Christmas kittens?"

"Did we really have a choice?" Sir joked.

"Of course, you did. You could choose to come of your own volition or wait until I hogtied you and brought you myself."

Sir smirked. "I thought as much."

"What's with all the Christmas decorations this year?" Brie asked as she walked inside and saw a beautiful Christmas tree by the fireplace.

"Shey reminded me of how much I liked the holiday growing up. I'd kind of forgotten that over the years. But, enough about the decorations. Come meet the new members of the family."

Sir raised his eyebrow as he looked at Brie. It did seem Master Anderson had already claimed them in his heart.

Cayenne and her two newborns were lying in a large cat bed next to the tree.

Brie knelt down on the floor to let Shadow go. He immediately joined Cayenne in the bed, settling down behind her, and began licking her fur.

"Oh, Shadow," Brie cooed in delight. "You two made two adorable tortoise shells, one with a pink nose and one with a black one. How cute is that?"

Master Anderson looked down at them like a proud papa. "They're damn cute, if I do say so myself."

Brie looked up at him. "Have you decided which one you are giving Shey?"

"I have," he stated with a grin. "What's better than one kitten?"

"Two!" Brie giggled, looking up at Sir who was shaking his head.

"What?" Master Anderson asked, elbowing Sir in the ribs.

"I told Brie you were keeping them."

"No, I'm giving both to Shey. Not the same thing at all."

"Right…"

"It's all about sharing the love of Christmas, man."

Brie looked down at the tiny kittens nestled against their mother with Shadow resting against Cayenne, his purrs filling the room.

These little Christmas kittens were a tiny miracle…

Brie smiled at Shadow, her heart bursting with joy.

Kinky Eve

Kinky Eve was a new event happening at the Submissive Training Center the night before Christmas Eve, and Brie was sad that Rytsar would not be attending the celebrations.

Sir, Marquis, and Faelan had organized a huge holiday-themed BDSM extravaganza as a charity event. Stephanie Conner, the young woman who headed Rytsar's Tatianna Legacy Center which served women rescued from sexual slavery, had been invited to accept the check.

The timing was unfortunate, however, because Rytsar had left a day earlier for Russia to visit Vlad's two-year-old son. Brie understood the importance of his trip, but she knew that she and all the submissives in attendance would deeply miss his presence.

Sir had been secretive about the event itself, leading Brie to speculate on what the three were planning.

The fact that they were holding it at the Training Center had her imagination running wild. Would it be a bunch of demonstrations to watch and enjoy while they ate a formal holiday dinner? Or, would it be a free-for-all where they would be allowed to use any room in the entire Center however they wanted? There was also the chance that the sole purpose was to invite the vanilla community in to mingle with them in a casual setting.

With the possibilities being limitless, and those three men at the helm, whatever it was would be extraordinary.

"How should I dress for tonight?" Brie asked, hoping to get a hint about the night's events.

"I would recommend the gown hanging in your closet."

Brie raced to her closet to find a long dark green dress, sparkly heels, and a sexy panty and bra set covered in candy canes and lace waiting for her.

"Thank you, Sir!" she cried as she immediately stripped out of her clothes and slipped on the panty set.

"The festive underwear is for me to enjoy later," he said seductively.

Based on his comment, Brie narrowed it down to a holiday dinner in the commons area of the school or a vanilla dinner to benefit the charity. Nobody came to the Center dressed up in formal clothing if they were planning to scene.

As Brie slipped on the flattering gown, she told Sir, "I can't tell you how excited I am that we are gathering at the Training Center. It will be such fun to celebrate the holidays with our friends."

"I agree, babygirl," he replied, straightening his green tie before buttoning up his black jacket. Looking at his watch, Sir said, "We'll be heading out soon to drop Hope off at my aunt and uncle's before we head to the Center."

"I won't be long," she assured him as he left.

Brie hurried to finish getting ready, taking one last look in the mirror, before leaving to grab Hope's overnight bag. She headed out the door behind Sir, curious what the night would hold.

Brie could hardly contain herself when they pulled up to the Training Center an hour later. "Every time I come here, I remember that first day and how nervous I felt when I walked into that building."

Sir held out his hand, helping Brie out of the car. "Are you ready to discover what lies inside for you tonight?"

"As much now as I was then, Master," she answered as he held out his arm to her and escorted her inside.

Rachael Dunningham, the first person Brie met on her first day of class, greeted them as they headed toward the elevator. "Merry Christmas, Sir Davis and Mrs. Davis."

"The same to you, Miss Dunningham."

"Aren't you going to join us downstairs?" Brie asked, sad at the thought of Rachael being stuck upstairs greeting guests while everyone else enjoyed the party below.

"I appreciate you thinking of me, Mrs. Davis, but there's no need to worry. Several of us volunteered to take shifts so no one misses out on the festivities."

"I'm so glad to hear that. I would love to spend time catching up with you after your shift is done."

Rachael glanced at Sir and smiled. "We'll see if there's time for that."

Brie took both her hands and squeezed them, promising, "I will make sure there's time."

Rachael nodded, smiling graciously. "I'll see you downstairs then."

Brie waved to her as the elevator doors opened and she stepped inside with Sir. Brie could hardly contain herself as the elevator headed down. When the doors opened, she let out a gasp.

The commons had been transformed into a winter scene with blue and silver cloth cascading from the ceiling and down over the walls while sparkling snowflakes hung from ceiling and twinkling pine trees lined the outer walls. In the back was a giant gold chair upholstered in red velvet with a large sack sitting beside it.

Elaborately decorated dining tables filled the center of the commons area, leading Brie to believe that she was right about the formal dinner.

"A charity dinner?" she asked Sir.

"Not exactly," Sir stated, stepping out of the elevator.

Two submissives dressed as sexy Christmas elves walked up to them.

"Is everything in place?" Sir asked them.

"I'm pleased to report that Santa has been working us elves very hard. You'll find everything as you wanted, Sir Davis."

"Good," he replied, sounding pleased.

Brie looked around at the beautiful decorations and stated. "I actually expected there would be a performance or a demonstration tonight."

"What would be the fun in that?" Faelan asked, coming up behind them.

Brie turned to see that his girlfriend, Kylie, was with him. She wore a royal blue dress, which perfectly matched the color of the eyepatch Faelan was wearing.

"Don't you two look stylish?" Brie said in admiration.

"I love getting dressed up for fancy occasions," Kylie confessed.

"And, I love undressing you," Faelan told her with a sly grin.

Brie found their easy relationship endearing.

"So, is this purely a holiday dinner with kinky friends?" Brie pressed Faelan.

He laughed. "Do you really think we would be that lame?"

Sir looked at him and said, "I haven't told her a thing."

Faelan winked at her. "Ahh…well, you are in for a surprise, then."

"Do you know?" Brie asked Kylie.

She shook her head. "No. I think all of us submissives have been kept in the dark."

Faelan wrapped his arm around Kylie's waist. "It was the only way to surprise all of you."

She grinned at him. "Well, I can't complain because I love surprises."

"I do too," Brie agreed, laughing. "I just don't have the patience to wait for them."

The elevator doors opened and Marquis walked out with Celestia beside him. She wore a silver gown that complemented Marquis' classic tux.

Marquis approached them wearing a rare smile. "I have great expectations for tonight."

"As do I," Sir agreed, pulling Brie closer.

"Why all the secrecy, Marquis Gray?" Brie

asked.

"Think of it like a magic trick, Mrs. Davis. If you knew all the components, it would lose its full impact."

"True," Brie conceded. Now she was even more excited about the evening ahead.

"When I heard they were planning this gathering, I was thrilled," Celestia said.

"Me, too," Kylie agreed. "I love holiday parties."

Brie addressed the three Doms, "I'm thrilled to be here tonight celebrating with my friends and the fact that Rytsar's recovery center is reaping the benefits of this evening makes it even more special."

"I agree, babygirl," Sir said. "However, this is not a simple gathering. I plan to challenge you tonight."

His declaration set her heart aflutter.

The elevator opened as the first of the guests arrived for the event. After all the guests had been seated, Sir escorted Brie to their table where she found Lea, Mary, Autumn, and Tono waiting for them.

Brie was thrilled to be sitting with some of her favorite people.

"Merry Christmas everyone!"

When Brie sat down, Lea grabbed her hand and squeezed it. "I'm so excited that I get to spend tonight with you, girlfriend!"

"Me too!" Autumn agreed.

Mary shrugged. "I'm not nearly as giddy as these two lug nuts, but MC back at ya, Stinks."

Brie grinned, happy to have Mary at the table.

Turning her attention to the Japanese Kinbaku Master, Brie bowed her head. "Tono, it is always a joy to see you."

His smile was gentle and kind. "I feel the same, Mrs. Davis."

It comforted Brie to know she still had a deep connection with Tono despite the different directions their lives had taken.

Marquis Gray walked to the front of the room to address the assembly. "We are grateful you have joined us tonight for our very first holiday gathering here at the Submissive Training Center."

Applause followed and someone yelled, "It's about time!"

Chuckles emanated from the crowd.

"I agree," Marquis stated. "And if things go well tonight, we will consider doing it again next year."

More applause followed.

"As far as the evening's events, each sub will receive a special booklet. As you complete each task, the page will be stamped. As with all BDSM scenes, you have a choice. In this case, you can either choose to participate or watch. That is completely up to you."

Brie's eyes widened as she looked around the room. She realized that many of the Doms in attendance were well known for their skills…

"We would like to thank you for the generous donations received thus far. If you are particularly pleased with an activity tonight, we ask that you show your gratitude by making an additional donation in honor of the Dominant who scened with you. We have a donation box set up over here."

He pointed to a white box covered in snowflakes and blue crystals set on a bright red stand.

"To start off our evening, we will begin with a variety of light tapas. As Master Gannon so eloquently once said, 'It's during meals that connections are made and cemented. We are not just a bunch of kinksters, but a true community in every sense of the word.'"

Everyone cheered.

Marquis raised his hands and servers appeared while holiday music started playing in the background.

Boa, the handsome submissive Brie had become friends during her training, came to each table and handed every submissive a pretty red bag with a gold drawstring.

Brie was about to open hers, but then asked Sir, "It is all right if I look at it now?"

He smiled knowingly. "You may, but had you failed to ask me, I would have spanked that pretty little ass of yours the minute you did."

She giggled as she opened the bag.

Taking out a small booklet, she flipped through the pages and saw that each page had a different holiday theme written on it. There were over twenty in all, including:

Candy Canes

Naughty or Nice

Christmas Lights

Present Tied with a Bow

Chestnuts Roasting

Carving the Goose

Whipped Cream Topping

Mistletoe Madness

While everyone enjoyed their meal, the girls discussed what they thought each one meant, much to the amusement of Sir and Tono.

Before the meal was over, Stephanie Conner walked up to speak to Sir.

"I just wanted to say how grateful I am that you chose the Tatianna Legacy Center as your charity tonight."

"There is no need to thank us," Sir told her. "It's an honor to contribute to it knowing the profound difference you are making to those rescued from that life."

Brie agreed, "You are saving lives, Stephanie."

Mary spoke up. "I've seen it with my own eyes while volunteering there. Your program gives the women purpose again. I cannot tell you how crucial that is."

Brie looked at Mary with compassion.

After all the abuse Mary had suffered at her father's hands, she understood better than Brie what these girls had endured.

"Mrs. Davis, I trust that you and the baby are doing well?" Stephanie asked, smiling at her.

Brie nodded. "We are."

"That's wonderful to hear."

But then, Brie sighed. "I'm just sad that Rytsar couldn't be here tonight. This would have meant so much to him. I hope you know nothing could have kept him away if he hadn't had to travel to Russia."

Stephanie smiled warmly. "I know."

Brie didn't think her respect for Stephanie could grow any stronger and told her, "You are living proof of what is possible after the horrors you faced. I want you to know how deeply I admire you."

Stephanie blushed. "No need to put me on a pedestal, Mrs. Davis. I wouldn't be here today if it hadn't been for Rytsar."

Brie smiled. "Your success brings him great joy."

Stephanie bowed slightly, blushing again. "I will excuse myself so you can finish your meal. I just wanted to express how much this event means to me, my staff, and the women it will help."

As Stephanie walked away, smiling and nodding to others as she returned to her seat, Brie thought back to the night in Russia when she had seen that same girl lying broken and abused on the ground being sold to the highest bidder.

Brie closed her eyes, forcing back the tears.

Rytsar risked his life to save her...

Opening her eyes, Brie looked at Stephanie again. The fact that the young woman was such a positive force in the world spoke to her incredible inner strength and the power of the human spirit.

Shortly afterward, Sir and Tono stood up and excused themselves from the table. Before Sir left, however, he leaned down and whispered in Brie's ear, "Save 'Chestnuts Roasting' for last, babygirl."

Her heart raced as she watched Sir leave, along with many of the Doms in the room.

Lea nudged her. "Any ideas yet about what 'Mistletoe Madness' is?"

"I haven't a clue, but it sure sounds fun," she giggled and pointed to her pamphlet. "This is where I'm headed first."

"Where's that?" Autumn asked.

Brie showed her the page as she read it out loud, "I'm headed to 'Present Tied with a Bow'. The second I saw Tono leave with the others, I knew that one had to be him."

"Wouldn't it be fun if we all went together?"

Lea grinned.

Brie loved the idea. "Oh, that would be *such* fun!"

"Count me out," Mary stated. "I like the rope freak and all…" She glanced at Autumn. "…no offense. But, I'm set on 'Carving the Goose'."

While they were talking amongst themselves, Boa stood up to address the entire group as a whole. "As you can see, the Masters have left to prepare for their scenes. Everyone is welcome to watch but, submissives, this night is all about you. You have the honor of choosing the scenes that interest you. Your only limit is your own curiosity. If you find a scene particularly enjoyable, we ask again that you consider donating to the Tatianna Legacy Center in that Master's name.

"If you choose to scene tonight, we have a clothing check in the first room down the hall on the left."

Someone raised their hand. "None of these are labeled in the booklet. How do we know where to go?"

Boa smiled. "That's part of the challenge."

"It's like a giant scavenger hunt!" Brie grinned.

Another person raised their hand. "Is it possible to complete them all?"

Boa chuckled. "No, there won't be enough time. But, listen for the bell. It will announce that the sessions will be ending soon and you should have time for one more."

"Please meet back here when you are finished. We have something very special planned to end our evening tonight."

Brie smiled down at her booklet wondering how many she could get through before she met up with Sir for the final bell.

Holiday Scenes

The four girls headed to the clothes check room and Brie, Lea, and Mary immediately stripped down to their underwear without giving it a second thought. Having trained together at this facility, they were used to seeing each other's bodies.

"Oh, look at your adorable underwear! Lea cried as Brie shimmed out of her green dress.

"Thanks! Sir bought them for me," Brie told her, turning to Lea. She immediately burst out in giggles when she saw what Lea was wearing.

Lea grinned, sticking out her chest to show off her bra. Each cup had Rudolf's face, complete with a red nose, big brown eyes, and antlers.

"You want to rub Rudolf's nose for good

luck?" Lea joked.

"Oh, Lord, you two," Mary grumbled. "You're like little kids."

Mary was wearing a very expensive black satin panty set.

Although Autumn was shy about undressing, she followed suit, removing her dress which exposed her artificial leg. Brie smiled to herself, grateful that Autumn didn't show any signs of discomfort or embarrassment even though she was among a bunch of strangers at the Training Center. She'd changed a lot under Tono's care.

When Mary saw Autumn's cute panty set with red velvet and furry white accents, she rolled her eyes. "I wouldn't be caught dead in Christmas lingerie."

"Why not?" Autumn asked with a smirk.

"You really need to get into the holiday spirit," Lea said, grabbing Brie and Autumn as she swung her hips from side to side, bumping them playfully. "Do you know why Santa is so freaking jolly?"

Mary frowned, knowing a joke was coming.

"Because he knows where all the naughty girls live!"

Brie giggled when she saw Mary's frown

deepen.

Autumn giggled at Lea's joke and then asked, "What do you call Santa's helpers?"

"Eep!" Lea squeaked, excited that Autumn was jumping in with a joke. "Tell me, tell me!"

"Subordinate clauses."

Lea and Autumn broke into hysterical laughter while Brie gave Mary an amused look.

"And…I'm out," Mary announced, turning away from them and walking down the hallway, looking absolutely stunning in her sexy black underwear and red heels.

"Poor Mary. She tries so hard to pretend she hates my jokes."

Pointing at Lea, Brie laughed. "That, right there, is your best joke yet, Lea."

"Giiiirl…I will pretend you did not just say that," Lea teased, giving Brie a nudge.

"I think we'd better find Tono before everybody else does," Autumn stated when she saw all the other submissives heading out.

Brie took off her high heels, holding them in one hand. "Fastest way to get there is without shoes."

The other two removed theirs and the three took off down the hall, giggling the entire way.

All the doors of the school were closed, but scattered throughout were signs on certain ones with one of the names of the Christmas themes.

Brie made a mental note of the ones she wanted to try next as they ran past them. Naturally, the room "Present Tied with a Bow" was on the far end of the school.

Luckily, they found they were the first ones there when they burst into the room. Their giggling instantly stopped when they stepped inside. The lights of the room were turned down low, but playful white Christmas lights lined the edge of the ceiling. In the center was a large jute mat with bundles of ropes in green and red laid out in a row. From the ceiling hung a large, multicolored metal ring that reflected the light from the white lights, making it glow like a star.

To top it off, the room was filled with the sound of Tono's familiar flute music, but for a fun twist, the melody was a simple Christmas song.

Autumn giggled. "Tono, I can't believe you pulled this off without me suspecting a thing."

Tono winked at her. "It was difficult to keep it a secret from you. However, it was worth it to see the surprise on your face when you walked in."

Brie smiled at Tono. "I love what you've done to this room!"

"I'm glad," he answered, his chocolate brown eyes twinkling with pleasure.

Breathing in the peace Tono inspired, Brie let out a contented sigh. Just being in his presence was a gift.

"Since the three of you came together, would you like me to tie you at the same time or separately?"

Brie remembered the sexy birthday present that Lea had given her when they'd shared in a scene with the Kinbaku Master. Without hesitation, she answered, "All together."

Both Lea and Autumn chimed in with their enthusiastic agreement.

"Excellent. Place your shoes by the door and join me on the mat."

Once Brie made her way over to the jute mat, Tono began tying a simple chest harness using the red rope. Brie smiled as the rope slid across her skin, tickling her.

Chest harnesses were both fun and beautiful. The tight constriction reminded Brie of a corset, and the way it enhanced the breasts was lovely and flattering.

Once each of them was similarly bound, Tono commanded, "Form a triangle by touching your shoulders together while facing away from each other."

Brie was intrigued as she stood facing Tono, her left shoulder pressing against Lea and her right against Autumn.

"Now, to create the vision while you use each other as support," Tono said, kneeling down at Brie's feet. He took her right leg and lifted it, pressing her ankle against her left knee and securing it in place with green rope.

Standing as they were, she was able to balance by leaning against the other two girls. He then moved to Autumn and did the same, carefully tying her ankle against her artificial leg. After finishing with Lea, he went back to Brie and told her to lift her arms up.

Tono started the process of securing her wrists together, their bodies mere inches from each other as he bound her wrists. The Kinbaku Master purposely teased her skin with the rope as he worked.

His close proximately made it easy for Brie to sync her breathing with his and, as soon as she found his rhythm and matched it, he paused what he was doing to smile at her.

There was no one in the world as skilled with jute as he was, and Brie silently thanked Sir for giving her, and all of the other submissives, this special gift.

Tono took the green rope that bound her wrists and slipped it through the ring above, pulling it tight to lift her hands high above her head.

"Beautiful," he commented once he'd finished and stood back to look at her.

Moving to Autumn, he took his time as he bound his submissive with the green rope, tying her in the same position as Brie.

Brie could see his smile as he picked up the rope for Lea and commanded her to lift her arms. There had been a time when Lea had served under Tono as his temporary submissive. Each of them had a special connection to Tono Nosaka, as well as to each other, which made this scene more intimate and fun.

After he was done, Tono walked around them and made slight adjustments while he admired the simple beauty he had created with their bodies and his jute.

Taking out his phone, Tono made a short video as he walked around them again. "I want you each to know how beautiful you look connected together."

A submissive entered the room and immediately bowed her head. "I'm sorry for disturbing you, Tono Nosaka. Should I leave?"

He stopped recording and smiled at her. "No, stay. We are almost done here."

With efficient yet sensual movements, Tono untied each of them, starting with Autumn and ending with Brie.

"Thank you, Tono," Brie said, bowing to him once she was free of his rope.

"It is always good to reconnect with you, toriko."

Her smile broadened. "I feel the same, Tono."

He stamped each of their booklets with their first stamp—a red orchid.

Before they left, he cupped Autumn's chin in his hand and gave her a tender kiss. "Have a good time tonight, *kohana*."

Brie's heart melted witnessing the love between the Master and sub.

Another submissive entered the room just

after Brie picked up her shoes to leave. Brie joined her friends in the hallway and said, "Something tells me Tono is going to be very busy tonight."

"There's no doubt about it," Lea said, laughing from the natural high his bondage evoked.

"I agree," Autumn answered, giggling, "but he truly loves what he does."

Brie nodded, smiling so hard it almost hurt. "That was the perfect way to start off this evening."

"Where to next?" Lea asked.

"Why not 'Mistletoe Madness' for Lea?" Autumn suggested. "I saw it on our way here and it's not too far."

"Sounds like a plan," Brie agreed.

"Thanks girls. You know, I've been dying to find out what it is…!" Lea exclaimed as she started running toward the room. "The faster we get there, the more sessions we can cram in."

Lea beat them to the door and opened it for them. "Brains before boobs," she said as they entered.

Brie tweaked Rudolf's nose as she passed by.

The room was bathed in red light and Brie was thrilled to see Baron was the Dom.

Glancing around the room, she noticed there were several observers standing in the back as two girls, who must have just finished their scene with him, stood up and bowed to Baron.

Baron commanded one of the girls to come to him. He leaned down to give the submissive a kiss and murmured, "Well done," in a low, seductive voice.

Brie spotted the mistletoe above his head and smiled to herself, understanding the first part of the scene's name. However, she had yet to figure out what the "Madness" was.

After the two girls left, Brie addressed Baron formally. "We are here to serve you, Baron."

His white teeth gleamed against his dark skin when he smiled. "Which scene did you just finish?"

Brie returned his smile. "We visited Tono Nosaka first."

"Ah…then I bet you all are feeling relaxed right now."

"We are, Baron," they answered in unison.

"Well, I'm about to change that," he said with a sexy smirk. "We are going to play a game, and whoever is the last to successfully meet my demands will be rewarded with a congratulatory kiss."

Brie knew Baron was quite the kisser and glanced at her friends, wondering which one of them would get a kiss from his sensual lips.

"What do we have to do to win your kiss, Baron?" Lea asked.

"It's simple, really." Baron walked over to a large green bag and pulled out three small boxes. "For this challenge, I'm giving you each a vibrator to keep. The first thing you must do is kneel on the mat and slip it under your panties, making sure it rests snuggly against your clit."

Up for the challenge, Brie and Lea quickly took the vibrators out of their boxes and knelt on the mat, both of them discreetly placing the toy as he had directed.

Baron helped Autumn to the floor and told her to find a position that was comfortable. She giggled nervously as she slipped the vibrator under her panties.

While Baron went to get them something else from the bag, Lea whispered to Autumn, "Nothing to be nervous about. Baron is all kinds of kinky fun."

He came back holding three large peppermint sticks in his hand.

Approached Brie first, he commanded, "Open."

Brie immediately opened her lips and he placed the rod in her mouth, commanding, "Hold it there, kitten, and do *not* let it drop."

The sweet flavor of peppermint tickled Brie's tongue as she nodded to acknowledge his command.

Once each of them was holding a peppermint stick in her mouth, Baron explained, "You only need to do two things to please me. Hold on to your peppermint and do not come."

When Lea groaned, Baron winked at her, adding with a sexy smile, "Naturally, I control your vibrators. The last sub to keep those two simple commands earns a kiss."

Brie looked up at him expectantly, waiting for the challenge to begin.

Baron smiled as he turned a central dial and their vibrators suddenly came to life. Autumn almost lost her peppermint right there, but quickly recovered.

Expecting Baron to turn up the vibration gradually, Brie was surprised when he purposely varied it. One moment the vibrator was slow and seductive, and the next it was vibrating full blast and rocking her clit.

Keeping her on her figurative toes like that made it easy for Brie not to come, but it was during one of those heavy vibration blasts that Autumn gasped and dropped her peppermint stick.

"I'm sorry, but you are out," Baron told her with a grin.

He now concentrated his full attention on Lea and Brie, adjusting the vibration to the perfect setting. With Brie's clit already stimulated by the varied vibrations, it responded hungrily to the constant rhythm that, with each burst of vibration, mimicked the timing of a cock thrusting into her pussy.

Brie moaned, enjoying it a little too much.

Lea turned her head and smiled at Brie with the large peppermint stick stil in her mouth. It was obvious that Lea thought she was going to win, which spurred Brie on to try even harder to beat her.

Closing her eyes, Brie focused her thoughts.

It was a hard-won battle between the two girls because they both were experienced in orgasm denial. Luckily for Brie, a group of girls came bursting into the room and caused Lea to lose her concentration. The peppermint stick fell to the floor as she let out a passionate cry of "Yes, yes, yes!" and climaxed.

Brie felt the thrill of victory when the vibration suddenly stopped. She stood up slowly, her pussy still throbbing from the ghostly vibrations of the toy.

Baron stamped each of their booklets, stating, "Enjoy the rest of the evening, ladies, and don't forget to take your new toys with you."

Brie retrieved her vibrator and put it back in the small box, slipping it into her red velvet bag.

She smiled when Baron beckoned her to come to him.

Lifting her chin, Brie stood on tiptoes to receive his enticing kiss.

"Well done, kitten," he murmured seductively.

Her heart swelled with pride until she realized that by winning, she had denied herself an orgasm, leaving her in a needy state.

Baron winked at her, knowing perfectly well the condition she was in.

Grabbing her shoes, she left the room with her pussy still aching with desire.

As soon as the door shut behind them, Lea

gave her a high five. "Well done, Stinky Cheese!"

Brie grinned, embracing her victory even though she was a quivering mess. "Thanks, Lea."

Autumn snorted. "It wasn't even a contest for me."

Lea put her arm around her friend. "Tell Tono you need to practice some orgasm denial."

"Nah…" she answered. "I like coming too much."

"I agree, Autumn," Brie said, biting her lip.

"Where to now, girls?" Lea asked.

"Why don't you pick this one, Autumn?" Brie suggested.

She looked at her booklet and smiled. "I think 'Christmas Lights' sounds sweet."

"'Christmas Lights' it is, then," Lea said, grabbing Autumn and Brie's hands as they headed down the hall together.

When they finally found the correct door, they entered the room quietly.

Instead of being filled with white Christmas lights as Brie had expected, this room had dark purple ones that produced a sexy ambiance.

"Oh, I love purple," Lea purred softly. When she saw the Dom running it, she whispered to the other two, "Who the heck is he?"

Brie smiled, remembering when Master Nosh had introduced her to Hunter during a special outing with Sir.

"His name is Hunter. I was told that he was the top student of his Dominant Training class."

"Oooh…" Lea said, ogling him more closely.

"I wonder what makes him the top of his class?" Autumn whispered.

"I don't know, but I think we are about to find out," Brie said as he dismissed the other submissives and motioned them forward.

"Bow to me," he ordered in a tone that commanded respect.

Brie immediately lowered herself to the floor and bowed, instinctually reacting to his dominance.

"Good," he told them. "Do you submit to me for this scene?"

Brie felt goosebumps rise on her skin in response to his question.

"Yes," she answered with the other two.

"You may stand and face your Master."

Brie heard Lea whimper excitedly.

There was definitely something different about Hunter that had each of them responding to his dominance.

"Stand with your back straight and your hands behind your neck."

Brie followed his directions, staring ahead even though she was tempted to check him out.

Hunter stood behind Autumn and tied a blindfold over her eyes. He moved to Lea next, and then to Brie. His aura of dominance was palpable, causing Brie's heart to race when he placed the blindfold over her eyes.

Once it was tightly secured, Brie felt more relaxed. Blindfolds always seemed to have that effect on her.

She felt him leave her side and waited patiently for his next command.

Suddenly, the distinctive electric buzz of a violet wand filled the air.

"Nod your head if any of you have felt a violet wand before," he stated.

Brie nodded, smiling slightly because she happened to enjoy the instrument.

Hunter walked over to Autumn first.

"So, this is your first time?" he asked. The low, sensual tone of his voice made Brie's stomach quiver even though he wasn't speaking to her.

"Yes," Autumn answered meekly.

"I will start out on a light setting and increase it slowly."

Brie heard Autumn gasp as the wand made contact with her skin, but then she began to giggle as she grew used to its ticklish touch. Hunter increased the level three times before turning off the instrument.

"Did you like that?" he asked her in a seductive tone.

Autumn sounded surprised when she answered, "Yes…"

"Yes, what?"

"Yes, Master."

"Good."

He moved on to Lea next. "You are familiar with my instrument?"

"I am, Master."

"Do you like it more intense?"

"I do," she answered breathlessly.

The violet wand began to buzz again. Brie could hear that the intensity was much higher, based on the sound it made on contact with Lea's skin. Instead of crying out, Lea moaned in pleasure.

"Higher?" he murmured lustfully.

"Yes, Master," Lea begged.

Brie stood stock still as she listened to the sensual exchange between Lea and Hunter as he continued to tease her with the violet wand.

Before Lea was ready for it to end, he turned off the instrument and she whimpered.

"I believe you would benefit from a longer session."

"I agree, Master," Lea answered.

Just like that, a future BDSM date had been set.

Brie's happiness for Lea was soon eclipsed by Hunter's presence as he moved to her. She felt chills when he murmured in her ear, "You are familiar with my instrument?"

"I am, Master," Brie answered, her attention now focused solely on him.

"Do you like it more intense?"

"Not as intense as my friend, Master."

It pleased her when she heard his low chuckle.

"Do you like to be challenged, sub?"

Brie answered truthfully, even though she was afraid of the consequences. "I do, Master."

"Then I will challenge you."

Brie's heart skipped a beat. She wondered what she had just gotten herself into. Thankfully, she could always call her safeword if things got *too* intense for her.

When the wand began to buzz, Brie could instantly tell by the sound that it was at a lower setting than what he used on Lea and she relaxed.

However, that all changed when he grazed the instrument against her sensitive stomach making her insides jump.

Hunter continued to graze the instrument against her skin, picking ever more sensitive areas such as the back of her knees, her inner thighs, her tailbone, her hard nipples, and then, finally, her neck.

By the time he was done, her skin was covered in goosebumps and she was quivering with an even greater need.

"Did you enjoy the challenge?" he asked in a gruff voice.

"Yes, Master. Very much."

"Good," he answered, undoing her blindfold.

He stood back to address all three. "I release you from my service."

Brie heard Lea sigh as he stamped her booklet and they turned to leave so the next set of submissives could take their place.

Once they were out of the room and at a safe distance away, Lea squealed. "O-M-G, is Hunter amazing or what?"

"He certainly is," Brie agreed excitedly. "I understand why Master Nosh holds him in such high regard."

Autumn nudged Lea. "And someone just got an invitation for a second round with him."

Lea grinned, her eyes flashing with excitement. "I about died when he said that."

Brie wrapped her arms around Lea. "I hope he knocks your socks off next time around."

Lea started fanning herself. "He already did, Stinky Cheese. If you were to push me with your little pinkie, I'd fall over right now."

"What's all the fuss about?" Mary asked, walking up to them.

"We just had an amazing session with Master Hunter," Autumn told her.

"What? Which one is he doing?"

"'Christmas Lights'," Autumn answered.

"Funny, I was going to skip that one because it sounded so lame."

"It's not lame at all," Brie assured her.

"Huh…I might have to give it a try after I hit 'Naughty or Nice'. I hear Mistress Lou is doing that one and she's particularly good at punishing naughty girls."

"That sounds just up your alley," Lea agreed.

"Where are you headed next?" Mary asked.

"I was thinking we could go to 'Whipped Cream Topping'. I'm figuring that has to be Master Anderson," Lea said.

"It's got to be," Brie agreed.

"We'd better head there now because time is running out," Autumn stated.

"You guys go on without me," Brie told them, wanting to spend time with Mary.

As they headed off, Mary got out her booklet and asked, "Which one are you looking at, Stinks?"

Brie looked over her shoulder and pointed to the top one. "I'm curious about 'Candy Canes'."

Mary turned around and wiggled her ass, showing off the pink stripes on her butt. "Marquis Gray at his finest."

"Nice stripes," Brie complimented. "What was 'Carving the Goose' about?"

Mary gave her an odd smile. "That's the next one you should go to, Stinks. Trust me."

She suddenly turned and walked away, stating, "You'll find the room next to the auditorium. I suggest you run. There's no time to waste."

Brie chuckled to herself.

So much for spending time with Mary…

Brie shrugged and made her way to 'Carving the Goose', wondering why Mary had been so adamant about it.

Unexpected Surprises

Boa stopped Brie in the hallway on her way to "Carving the Goose" and asked, "Are you having fun, Brie?"

"I'm loving it, Boa! What about you?"

"It's been amazing so far. Where are you headed next?"

"I thought I'd try 'Carving the Goose'."

"Oh, that one is great—it's going to blow your mind."

"Really?"

"Oh, yeah." He chuckled. "Definitely can't miss that one."

"Which one are you headed to?"

"I'm feeling a real craving for 'Whipped Cream Topping'."

Brie grinned, knowing firsthand how much

Boa enjoyed the bullwhip. "Lea and Autumn are headed that way, too. Maybe you can catch up with them."

"Catch you later," he said, walking faster in that direction.

Hurrying herself, Brie finally found the right room and was shocked when she opened the door and saw who was running it.

Faelan looked up from four subs he was playing with and nodded to her. Brie shut the door quietly and stood watching him, curious now about how it went down for him when his ex, Mary, showed up for the scene.

Unlike the other holiday rooms, this one was brightly lit. Lights on the floor produced stripes of blue against the walls. For background music, Faelan had chosen dubstep versions of Christmas songs. Brie loved the beat of the hard base of Capital Kings amping up one of her favorite tunes, "Carol Of The Bells".

The edgier music went perfectly with his instrument of choice tonight—a blade.

The subs were all blindfolded. Brie knew that it would make the scene that much more intense for them—not knowing where he would drag the knife across their skin.

Faelan was highly experienced with knives and could leave light scratches on the skin or even deeper ones that would sting but not draw blood.

As she watched, she was struck by how dashing Faelan looked with his new eyepatch. But what caught her attention more was the expression on his face as he played with the subs. It was obvious by his smile that he enjoyed the thrilling fear he evoked from the submissives with his blade.

The girls continually gasped and cried out, but not one of them called their safeword. He had them eating out of his hand.

"Mrs. Davis, I need you to step out of the room for a moment," Faelan stated quietly.

Surprised by the request, Brie nodded to him and left, curious as to why she had been asked to leave. Suddenly, Brie heard cries of nervous laughter. A few moments later, the girls, all smiling, left the room looking at each other in disbelief.

What the heck had Faelan done to garner that kind of reaction?

When Brie reentered the room, she found herself alone with the Dom.

"What just happened?" she laughed.

He smiled charmingly. "Just a little friendly knife play."

"Well, everyone is raving about your scene."

"Would you like to experience it yourself, blossom?" he asked, pointing to the chair beside him. "Come, sit in my chair and let me do wicked things to your body."

There was a time when she would not have trusted him, but things had changed between them. She trusted Faelan with her life now and stepped up to the chair without hesitation.

"I enjoyed my scenes with you here at the Training Center," she told him as she sat down.

"As did I, blossom."

Faelan picked up a dangerous looking knife and informed her, "I promise not to cut you, but it will hurt. Do you consent?"

Tingling with fear, but still curious, Brie nodded.

"Do you remember that time when I used a blade on you?"

Chills crept over her skin as she thought back on it. "I do."

"Good."

He set the knife down and picked up a blindfold. "I know how much you love these."

She smiled, giggling nervously. "I do, but maybe not so much right now."

"Trust me," he stated confidently as he covered her eyes.

Brie sat there anxiously, wondering where she would first feel the sharp blade on her skin, and concentrated on the dubstep music, trying to keep her nerves down.

"I am going to drag this blade across your skin, but I will not draw blood unless you move. It is extremely important you do not move this entire scene. Do you understand?"

"I do, Faelan."

"Excellent..." he stated huskily, moving closer to her.

Even though he said he would not cut her skin, it felt like he was doing so whenever she felt the sharp knife drag across her thighs, back, and chest. She swallowed hard several times, unwilling to call her safeword because she found it fearfully erotic.

"You have done well, so let me challenge you now."

Brie heard him move away and put down the blade. Her breaths came faster when she heard him pick up something else.

"Are you ready?"

She nodded nervously, her breaths now coming in short gasps.

When he cut the skin across her stomach, the sting of it caused her to bite her lip to stop herself from crying out.

"Good girl," he murmured, lifting her blindfold to show Brie what he held in his hand.

She stared at the white feather, confused. Looking down at her bare stomach, she saw nothing, not even a scratch.

Brie looked up at him. "What did you do?"

Faelan chuckled. "I gave you exactly what you were expecting."

Brie looked at the feather again and laughed. "How did you make it feel so real?"

"Do you really want to know?"

"Please!"

"For tonight's scene, I've been using dull knives to be safe. Working with so many subs in one sitting, I wasn't willing to take the risk. Can you guess how I made it feel sharp?"

Fascinated, Brie shook her head. "Tell me."

He pulled a knife out from an insulated bag. "I keep the dull knives cold. Before the scene starts, I show each sub the large, sharp blade and then I blindfold them. When they feel the cold steel of the dull knife against their skin, their minds automatically associate it with the knife they just saw and they feel it cutting their skin."

"That reminds me of my branding at the Center, I swear I thought it was real. Even after I saw there was no brand on my skin, I could still feel the burn of it. How crazy is that?"

"The mind is a beautiful playground," he stated.

"I remember Sir telling me the same thing."

"He is an excellent teacher and I still utilize the lessons he taught me when I was starting out."

Faelan ran his cold blade against her thigh again and Brie smiled. "I would totally believe that was a sharp blade cutting me if I didn't know better."

"Especially when I pick a place that's extra sensitive, like this…" He ran it across her throat and Brie shivered with fear.

"Even knowing it can't hurt me, that was freaky," she confessed.

Faelan gave her a satisfied smile. "It's all in the delivery, blossom."

"Amazing that you went from a knife to a feather at the end," she laughed.

"Most subs react the way you did. Their minds are so set on the idea that I am holding a blade, that that's exactly what they feel. I can't tell you the number of subs who actually cry out in pain." He chuckled with amusement. "But, the kicker is when I take off their blindfold and show them the feather that just 'cut' them."

"That has got to be fun."

He raised an eyebrow. "Oh, it is. I enjoy a good mindfuck."

The bell rang announcing the sessions were about to come to a close.

"I'm sorry to leave you, Faelan, but I was told to meet Sir for the last scene."

"No reason to apologize. He's the one who came up with this event, after all."

Brie frowned slightly, confused by his statement. "What do you mean?"

"He approached Marquis with the idea for this Kinky Eve event."

"Wow, I didn't know that—thank you, Faelan, for everything."

"Anytime, blossom."

Brie left the room feeling as if she was walking on cloud nine as she hurried to meet up with her Master. She couldn't believe that the man who disliked Christmas had created all this—for her.

When she opened the door to the "Chestnuts Roasting" room, she found Sir performing fire play between two subs lying on separate tables, while a crowd of people lined the room to watch.

With reverence, she knelt down on the floor where he could see her and silently observed her Master while he made the flames dance across their bodies.

Brie considered fire play an art form on multiple levels—the wielder deciding the visual patterns and intensity of the flames while also considering the level of heat the sub would experience.

She loved fire play with Sir—and so, apparently, did a lot of other subs based on the number of people in the room.

After he finished the scene, Sir announced, "I apologize to those who have yet to scene tonight, but I am ending my session early." He looked over at Brie. "My sub has just arrived and I promised the last scene to her."

Brie's heart melted when Sir held out his hand and helped her to her feet. With a charming smile, he asked, "Are you ready to burn, babygirl?"

"Yes, please."

Brie trembled with excitement as Sir slowly took off her bra and panties and then bound her curls up in a hair tie while everyone else watched.

Sir kissed her on the cheek before ordering, "Lay face down on the table, téa."

Brie felt the butterflies start as she moved to the table and lay down. She loved the feel of the fiery heat just before Sir swept the flames away.

Although it took profound trust in a Dom to submit to such dangerous play, Brie did it enthusiastically, having experienced Sir's expertise multiple times.

Sir traced a line up her right thigh with his fingers before picking up the swab soaked in alcohol and following the same line he had just traced. The coolness of the alcohol caused goosebumps to rise on her skin.

He lit the slow-burning match in front of her and smiled as he moved into place. He then tapped the base of the line with the flame. Brie moaned in pleasure as the fire raced up the trail he'd just made.

Just before the heat became too intense, Sir swept it away with his hand. Her pussy contracted in pleasure when he slapped her ass playfully afterward.

Sir traced a trail up her other thigh with his fingers. "Do you want more, téa?"

"Yes, Master," she moaned.

He grazed the swab over the invisible line he'd just drawn and tapped the end with the fire, murmuring huskily, "Burn, baby, burn."

With another sweep of his hand and a swat on her ass, he had her craving more.

"I believe your ass needs my special attention."

Brie purred, nodding in agreement.

Sir caressed her bare ass with his free hand before giving her a forceful swat. Brie squeaked in surprise as tingles of pleasure shot straight to her groin. She moaned passionately, wanting more.

Where his hand made contact, the alcohol soon followed. Sir tapped her left ass cheek with the match and spanked the flames out with his hand.

"Oh…!" Brie cried out in pleasure, enjoying the erotic tingles his spanking created. Having been in an aroused state for most of the evening, Brie was crazy with desire.

Sir moved on to her right cheek, caressing it lovingly before following it up with the burning flames. Brie moaned even louder this time when he spanked away the flames.

He waited a few seconds before giving her another well-placed swat. Immediately, the tingles ignited, making her needy and wet.

She bit her lip when he said, "Whenever I think of Christmas, I see a log burning in the fireplace."

He trailed the swab slowly up her backbone, stopping just below her shoulder blades. This time, after tapping it with the match, he let the flames dance a little longer before sweeping them away.

The people watching their performance enjoyed the mystical allure of the flames and clapped in appreciation.

Sir had Brie completely entranced by the thrill of his touch and the heat of the flames. She never wanted it to stop, although she knew the end of the session was drawing near.

She closed her eyes and smiled when he traced his hand over her skin. Leaning down, he whispered to her, "What did I just draw on your back?"

Having concentrated solely on the pleasure of the scene, Brie had failed to take notice. She shook her head slightly.

"See if you can figure it out."

Using the cotton swab, he faithfully retraced the invisible line he had drawn before lighting her on fire.

The infinity symbol.

He had drawn the infinity symbol to end their session together. No one else would understand the significance but her.

Condors forever…

The people in attendance clapped as he blew out the match and thanked them for coming. As they filed out of the room, Sir covered her with his jacket.

"I ended our session early to give you time to bask in the afterglow before we rejoin the others."

"Thank you, Master." She smiled up at him and murmured, "Condors forever."

He winked at her as he cleaned up and put

away his tools.

Brie lay there in submissive bliss, watching him as he worked. "I will never forget this night," she told him.

"I'm glad you enjoyed it."

"Just so you know, I'm going to donate a million dollars in your name to the center."

He laughed. "Maybe you should wait on that one."

"You deserve that and more, Sir."

He walked over to her and kissed her lightly on the lips. "All I need is to know that you are happy, and you look happy right now."

"I am, Sir."

Sexy Santa

They were a little late when they joined the party in the commons. They found everyone enjoying a variety of desserts as well as after-dinner drinks by the time they arrived.

Brie slowly sat down next to Sir, still flying on a sub high. She found she couldn't stop smiling.

"You're freaking me out, Stinks," Mary muttered, taking a sip of her rum and Coke.

"Ah, leave her alone," Lea said. "She's just happy."

"Exactly. I can't handle overly happy people," Mary grumbled.

Brie reached out to take Mary's hand. "I love you, Mary."

Mary looked at her in surprise. "Ah…okay."

She laughed uncomfortably as she looked at the other people at the table and muttered, "Love ya, too, Stinks."

Brie grinned.

Marquis Gray gestured for Sir and Faelan to join him at the front while he addressed everyone. "Donations are still coming in, so we will give you a final total at the end of the night." He put his hand to his heart. "But, let me say that your generosity has been overwhelming." He looked over at Stephanie Conner and nodded.

Brie knew by Marquis's reaction that it must be a very impressive amount.

Sir raised his hands and clapped to everyone to show his appreciation. Brie smiled at him, her heart bursting with pride, knowing now that he was the one who had conceived this whole idea.

Faelan spoke up. "To thank you for your generosity, we have a special guest who has come a long way to be with us tonight. You may have heard of him…" He gestured to the hallway. "Let's give it up for the man who makes everyone's dreams come true."

People started clapping when Santa Claus rounded the corner with the two sexy elves at his side, while the sexy song "Santa Baby" played in the background.

Brie smiled at Lea and Autumn and the three stood up to cheer Santa on.

Santa waved at everyone at the tables as he made his way to the gold chair covered in red velvet. When he sat down, his two elves took their places to either side of him and he placed his hand possessively on the big green sack beside his chair.

"Do you know why Santa's sack is so big?" Lea asked.

Autumn looked at Lea and giggled as they both answered, "Because he only comes once a year!"

Mary piped up, "Damn, he must have some serious blue balls."

Brie started laughing hysterically, which caught Santa's attention, as well as everyone else in the room.

The jolly old man whispered to one of his elves, who walked over to their table. "Santa noticed someone being naughty at this table and commands you to go to him and receive your punishment."

Brie blushed, now suddenly silent as a mouse.

"I'll take her punishment," Lea offered, waving enthusiastically at Santa. "After all, it was my joke that caused her to laugh."

The elf looked back at Santa, who shook his head slowly.

"I'm sorry, no substitutes. It must be you," she stated, looking directly at Brie.

Hoping to avoid punishment, Brie stood up and said loud enough for everyone to hear, "I'm sorry for causing a disturbance, Santa. It won't happen again."

Santa gestured to her to come to him.

Brie looked back at Sir nervously before following the elf to Santa.

While Santa waited for her to make her way, he whispered something to his other elf.

When Brie arrived, the second elf told her, "Santa says you must lie on his lap to receive your spanking."

All the submissives in the room twittered excitedly, probably wishing they were her. But the idea of a public spanking made Brie antsy, even if it was being done in fun.

"I'm sorry, Santa."

Santa patted his lap.

With everyone watching her, Brie glanced at Sir, who nodded. Submitting to her punishment,

Brie bit her lip as she lay across Santa's lap.

Brie felt his gloved hand rub her ass several times before he lifted it to spank her. Brie closed her eyes, hoping she wouldn't make a fool of herself when his hand fell.

"*Radost moya…*"

Brie's eye popped open just as he smacked her hard on the ass and she cried out.

The entire room broke out in laughter.

"Rytsar?" She looked up at Santa and saw those mischievous blue eyes twinkling wickedly at her.

Before she could say another word, he spanked her again, evoking another painful cry of surprise, but Brie didn't care. She turned in his lap and wrapped her arms around his neck, his whiskers tickling her face.

"You are such an evil Santa!"

"*Da*," he agreed. "The evilest."

"Have you been here the whole night?"

He nodded, chuckling, "I was needed to keep everything running."

"All night long I've been mourning the fact you weren't here, and you were here the whole time?"

She could see his smirk under the beard.

"What can I say? I like grand entrances."

Brie buried her head in his white beard and hugged him even tighter.

"Would you like to help me pass out presents, naughty girl?"

She lifted her head to gaze into his intense blue eyes. "If it pleases you, Santa Rytsar."

He chuckled as he lifted her off his lap and then stood up, announcing in his Russian accent, "Everyone, I come bearing gifts. No one leaves here tonight without a present from the red man himself."

Brie looked over to where Sir was sitting and saw him smiling at her.

She mouthed the words, "I love you."

After all the presents had been passed out and the desserts had been consumed, Marquis came over with the final count, insisting Sir be the one to announce it.

Sir looked at the paper and raised his eyebrows. He stood up and made his way to the front.

"Miss Conner, would you please come up and join me?" he asked.

Stephanie walked up to Sir and smiled graciously as she stood beside him. Brie noticed, however, that her eyes were locked on Santa the entire time while Sir spoke.

"Before everyone heads out, we wanted to give you the final total for tonight."

Master Anderson started a drum roll at his table.

"Adding up the ticket prices, the general donations, and the ones made in honor of Doms here tonight, you have managed to raise over $124,000 for the Tatianna Legacy Center."

Everyone broke out in a roar of applause.

As Brie clapped, she smiled and thought to herself, *Plus one million in honor of Sir.*

When the last of the guests were leaving, Brie started to clean up.

Rytsar, who was still dressed as Santa—minus the beard—demanded, "What are you doing, *radost moya*?"

"The more people that help, the less everyone has to do," she answered.

He grabbed her wrist and forced her to put the decoration back down. "Hired workers will do that. Do not take away their livelihood."

"Okay…fine," Brie laughed. "I'll collect my things so we can leave, then."

Rytsar rode back with them, having hitched a

ride with Faelan to the Submissive Training Center earlier.

"How did you stay hidden the whole night?" Brie asked.

"I entertained myself with the two elves while my minions reported back to me. I heard you were one of the winners of Baron's challenge."

Brie giggled. "I was…unfortunately. Curse my competitive spirit."

Rytsar chuckled. "Feeling a little needy, are we?"

Brie looked at Sir and confessed, "I almost came during my scene with you."

Sir smirked. "I could tell, babygirl. I was sorely tempted to brush my finger against your clit."

Brie shivered pleasantly, her pussy pulsing with need from just thinking about his touch. "I'm definitely a level ten out of ten in neediness right now."

Both men glanced at each other, saying nothing.

Brie bit her lip as they pulled into the driveway. She hoped relief would be coming soon when Sir asked Rytsar to stay for a nightcap.

Rytsar agreed but insisted they sit on the couch while he got the drinks.

"Did you open the gifts I gave you both tonight?" Rytsar demanded, handing them each a shot glass.

"No. We didn't have any time to," Brie explained.

Rytsar frowned. "It is rude to leave gifts unopened when Santa is present."

"But, it's not even Christmas yet. Don't you want us to wait?"

"*Nyet.*"

Brie grinned. "Well, I have to admit I like the way you think."

Sir nudged him. "You do realize I'm trying to teach her patience."

"I do." He smirked.

"Fucking sadist."

"I wear the badge proudly, *moy droog.*"

Brie went to the car and came back with two small boxes, handing Sir the larger of the two which was addressed to him.

"Go ahead, *radost moya*. Open it," Rytsar commanded excitedly.

She smiled as she tore into the paper of the tiny box, wondering what it could be since his gifts tended to be extravagant. Lifting the lid, she smiled as she took out a silver toe ring with a white flower in the center.

She admired the pretty white petals and the bright yellow center and gave him a hug.

"This is lovely, Rytsar. Thank you."

When she pulled away, Rytsar sighed, taking off his Santa hat. His expression suddenly became serious. "After everything that's happened this year, I've had a profound epiphany, *radost moya*. Material things do not matter. It's not about what you can buy, but what you can give. When I saw this, it made me smile. I hope when you wear it, it will make you smile, too."

Brie hugged it to her chest before slipping it on the index toe of her left foot. "It'll make me smile every day when I look at it."

"I agree with you about the gifts," Sir told him. "It's one of the reasons I don't care for this holiday. A simple gift given in love is worth far more than anything money can buy."

"Well said, brother. Now, open my gift."

Sir tore at the paper and pulled out a set of black leather gloves. He studied them curiously.

"You don't like the gloves?" Rytsar asked, sounding slightly offended.

"It's not that I don't like them, but I don't wear gloves when I scene."

"Well, maybe you should."

Sir nodded, putting them on. "They are comfortable," he admitted.

"*Da*, and they make women go crazy. Just look at *radost moya*. She can barely keep her hands off you."

Brie giggled. "It's true, Sir. I'm crazy about you."

Sir cupped her chin with his gloved hand and kissed her hard on the lips.

"See? They are like magnets for the pussy," Rytsar asserted.

Sir chuckled, taking them off and placing them back in the box. "When I use them, I'll let you know what I think."

"Perfect," Rytsar said.

"Unfortunately, you'll have to wait for your gift, old friend. We don't open presents early in this house."

Rytsar shrugged. "It matters little to me. As I said, it's what you can give that counts."

He glanced at Brie hungrily. "And I am in the mood to give generously, over and over until you beg Santa for mercy."

Brie's desire shot through the roof when Sir replied, "Should we move this to our bedroom, then?"

"*Da.*"

She was trembling with excitement as she followed the two men. After a night of kinky teasing she was in desperate need of release!

"Let Rytsar undress you, then lie on the bed, téa."

Goosebumps rose on her skin as Rytsar unzipped her green dress and let it fall to the floor. He chuckled when he saw her festive panty set. "Your ass is covered in candy canes, r*adost moya.*"

She smiled. "Isn't it cute? Sir gave them to me as a gift."

Rytsar snorted. "It's good to see you have a sense of humor, *moy droog.*"

Sir looked at Brie lustfully. "I happen to enjoy the taste of peppermint."

Brie blushed, remembering the time he gagged her with a large peppermint stick.

Rytsar unclasped her bra next and tossed it to the floor, cupping her breasts in his big hands. Leaning down, he bit her neck, sending delightful chills through her body.

After slipping off her panties, he swatted her ass. "To the bed, woman."

Brie smiled at Sir as she climbed onto the bed

and lay down, her nipples already tight buds and her pussy soaking wet. She was so ready for this!

Rytsar lay down beside her, still dressed in his costume and smiled wickedly. "Tonight, I watch."

Brie raised her eyebrows in surprise and looked over at Sir.

"So be it." Loosening his green tie, Sir laid it on the nightstand.

Brie watched in rapt attention as he unbuttoned his shirt and shrugged it off. Piece by piece, Sir undressed in front of her, slowly exposing his sexy body. Even before he lay on the bed, she ached to be claimed by him.

Based on the hardness of his cock, it was obvious that Sir was in an equal state of arousal.

"Oh, Master..." she murmured. An electric current coursed through her when she felt his touch.

Sir claimed her lips roughly, his tongue penetrating her mouth. Brie moaned as he kissed her passionately, her body burning with desire, needing to feel him inside her.

"Please," she begged.

Normally, he would make her wait but, tonight, Sir seemed especially ravenous for her.

Moving between Brie's legs, Sir pressed his cock against her swollen pussy. She coated him with her wet excitement.

Arching her hips, she beckoned to him with her body, inviting him to claim her now.

"Please," she begged again.

He could not ignore her need and thrust into her.

Brie cried out in pleasure as he filled her with his cock.

Sir groaned in satisfaction as he forced her body to take his full length.

"Yes!" she screamed—needing and wanting to be fucked hard.

Brie looked up and met his gaze, reveling in the raging lust she saw in his eyes.

Images of their fire play danced in her head as he rammed his cock into her, showing her pussy no mercy.

When Rytsar started teasing her ass with his finger, her entire body clenched as a tremendous climax took away all thought. Brie momentarily lost touch with reality as she experienced a long and powerful orgasm.

Sir groaned, unable to control his own release because of the strength of hers. Brie's eyes fluttered and she was unable to voice a sound.

In that moment, he threw his head back and growled, "Fuck...!" as he came.

Brie had tears in her eyes when her climax finally ended.

"What was that?" she gasped breathlessly. "I think I just had the come of the century."

"It was quite impressive to watch," Rytsar stated, his eyes glinting with intense desire.

Sir rolled off Brie and lay there panting. "Holy fuck..." he groaned.

"Was it as good...for you...as it was for me?" she asked, still panting herself.

He turned toward her, his body drenched in sweat. "I came so hard that my balls still ache."

Brie gave him a gratified smile and turned her head to see Rytsar stroking himself through his Santa suit.

It was damn sexy.

"May I, Santa?" she asked.

Rytsar removed his hand.

Although still weak from her orgasm, Brie moved into position and freed his cock, taking his hard shaft into her mouth. His manly groan caused her pussy to contract in pleasure.

Needing to come again, Brie asked Sir,

"Would you play with me, Master?"

Sir smiled as he moved closer to her, reaching between her legs. Her pussy seemed extra sensitive to his touch, and she purred on Rytsar's shaft in excitement.

While she took her time and leisurely loved on Rytsar's cock, Brie came three more times. During her last orgasm, Rytsar grabbed her head and held it in place as he pumped his seed deep into her throat.

When she pulled away with his come coating her lips, she murmured seductively, "Oh, how I love the taste of Santa."

Christmas Morn

Brie woke up while it was still dark outside and smiled. She was bursting with excitement, knowing it was Christmas morning.

She rolled over slowly, not wanting to wake Sir, and was surprised to see he wasn't in bed.

"Sir?" she called out.

Silence.

As she walked out of their bedroom, she saw the light in the kitchen was on. Walking to the kitchen, she noticed Sir stirring a small pot on the stove.

"What are you doing up so early?" she asked playfully.

He turned to see she was still naked and smiled, holding his hand out to her. "Dressed in my favorite outfit, I see…"

Brie came to him and purred when he wrapped his arm around her. "You told me once that your family made hot chocolate together—a special cocoa that your mother reserved only for Christmas morning," he stated as he stirred the pot. "I had special chocolate delivered from Italy so I could treat you to a cup of hot chocolate that my *nonna* is famous for."

As Brie looked into the pot at the warm milk chocolate, tears came to her eyes. She had once surprised him with Ribollita on Christmas morning as her Christmas gift to him, and here he wanted not only to connect to her family's traditions but also to give her a taste of his.

She squeezed him hard, deeply moved by the gift. For a man who didn't care for the holiday, Sir truly knew how to give her the perfect present.

Once he'd poured the warm chocolate into two mugs, he sprinkled cinnamon on top. Before giving it to her, he turned on some music at a low volume. The sound of Alonzo's violin filled the kitchen as he played a soulful and poignant version of "What Child is This".

"Oh, my..." she whispered in awe, turning to Sir. "His violin is truly magical."

Sir smiled at her tenderly. "My father privately recorded a Christmas album for family and friends as his Christmas gift to them. I haven't listened to it since he died."

Brie closed her eyes, focusing on the emotion behind the instrument. Despite the fact that Alonzo was no longer on this Earth, the emotions he'd poured into his instrument were as alive now as they were the day he recorded it.

"He's here with us," she said, overcome with emotion.

Sir nodded with tears in his eyes. "Yes, he is. It feels as if he is speaking to me directly through his music." He handed her a mug as he took a drink himself.

Brie took a sip and moaned in pleasure. His *nonna's* hot chocolate was rich and thick, and the hint of cinnamon enhanced the flavor. "It's like drinking a melted bar of the most exquisite chocolate I've ever tasted."

"Nonna believes in feeding the soul with her cooking."

Brie smiled. "I consider my soul well fed today."

"Nonna would be pleased," he said with a smile.

They finished the chocolaty cup of love without speaking as they listened to Alonzo quietly serenading them with his violin.

Once she was done, Sir kissed her deeply. He tasted of chocolate as he explored her mouth with his tongue. It was decadent and sensual, making Brie purr in pleasure.

He broke the kiss and murmured, "I want you."

Those three words made her heart race. Taking her hand, Sir led her outside to their private hot tub. The sun was just breaking and coloring the sky with its pink hue. Brie shivered in the cold morning air, her nipples contracting into tight buds as he led her to the hot tub that he had already prepared.

Taking her hand, Sir helped her climb the steps and settle into the bubbling water.

"Wait...is that mint I smell?"

Sir smiled as he undressed to join her. "I added candy cane aromatherapy crystals to the water."

Tickled by the idea, Brie cupped the water and brought it to her nose, taking in the minty scent. "I love it, Sir."

He settled in beside her, stating lustfully, "I

want you to associate candy canes with being thoroughly fucked on Christmas."

Sir pulled her to him, claiming her mouth as his hands ran over her body. Brie melted against him, enjoying the heat of the bubbling water contrasting with the cool morning air.

That contrast alone was stimulating, but when she felt how hard his shaft was as it pressed against her, it made Brie that much hotter.

Sir lifted her and told her to straddle him as he pressed his cock against her pussy. Brie reached down and guided the head of his shaft into her, moaning as he penetrated her.

He put his finger to her lips. "Remember, there may be early risers out on the beach."

Brie's eyes widened. She had momentarily forgotten that someone might hear them. She nodded, blushing.

Sir took his finger away and ravaged her mouth while she ground against his hard cock. Brie's nipples rubbed against his chest as she rode his cock, sending her body into ecstasy.

She looked up at the sky streaked with colors. At the same time, the scent of peppermint filled the air and her thoughts.

Merry fucking Christmas to me!

Changing position, Sir moved behind her. The strategically placed "seat" of the tub had Brie at just the right height for her to lie on her stomach against the rounded edge of the hot tub while the jet stimulated her pussy.

Sir thrust his cock into her and she let out a muffled squeak, enjoying the strength of the thrust. Brie concentrated on the delicious combination of his deep penetration mixed with the intensity of the jets against her clit.

"Let's come together," he whispered huskily.

"I want nothing more, Master," she moaned, excited at the thought.

"I'm going to count down slowly when I am ready to come."

She only nodded in answer, trying desperately to stay her orgasm until his release.

"Look back at me, Brie," he commanded.

Looking back to meet his gaze, she watched as Sir slowed down his thrusts so her body could concentrate on his movements. With precision, he rubbed the head of his shaft against her G-spot.

She held her breath, chills of anticipation coursing through her body as he started to count down.

"Three…two…one…"

Her eyes never left his as her inner muscles squeezed his cock and he came inside her.

She was overcome by the love and passion in his gaze as they climaxed together. It was such an intimate and glorious feeling.

Afterward, he leaned down and kissed her. "Maybe it's time we start thinking about baby number two."

Brie's heart thrilled at the thought.

Sir stood up and reached over, grabbing one of the large beach towels he had laid out for them. He held it up for her and helped her out of the hot tub, wrapping her in the fluffy towel.

"Merry Christmas, babygirl."

She stood on tiptoes to kiss him on the lips. "Thank you for the best start to Christmas I could imagine."

"It's about to get even better," he stated, wrapping the other towel around himself. "Once we clean up, we're going to wake Hope and experience the magic of Christmas through our daughter's eyes."

Brie couldn't wait!

After they dressed, the two walked into

Hope's room together and Sir turned on the light.

Hope squirmed in her crib and slowly opened her eyes.

"Merry Christmas, my little angel," Sir said tenderly, smiling down at her.

Hope broke out in a grin and held her hands out. Brie picked her up and gave her a kiss on the cheek. "Here's to the first of many Christmases, sweet pea."

She carried her to the Christmas tree and settled down on the floor while Sir turned on the lights on the tree and set them to twinkling.

Hope's eyes widened as she stared at it. Her joy only increased when Shadow appeared and sat next to Brie. "Dow!"

Brie petted the cat as she looked at Sir, smiling.

"Which present do you want to unwrap first?" Sir asked Hope, pulling three presents out from under the tree.

Hope grabbed for the one with the red bow.

"This one it is, then," he said, sliding it over to her.

Brie pulled off the bow, gave it to Hope, before she slowly unwrapped the box. "Oh, look, sweetie. It's a stuffed teddy bear."

She was touched that Sir had purchased the gift himself, after examining a multitude of teddy bears at different stores.

"Feel how soft he is," Brie said, rubbing the soft fur against Hope's cheek.

Hope smiled but her attention was immediately drawn back to the red bow in her hand.

"Why don't you open the big box?" Brie suggested to Sir.

With great fanfare, Sir tore the paper and let it flutter to the ground. He opened the box itself and pulled out an activity table with tons of fun things to press, pull, and twist. He pressed a big yellow button and the funny noise it made caused Hope to laugh.

"That's more like it," Sir said, setting it next to her. Hope hit the button with her left hand and squealed in laughter, clapping her hands together when it made the sound again. In her excitement, she'd dropped the bow.

Once again, she focused on it as she picked it back up.

Sir chuckled, handing the last one to Brie. "Let's see if this last one will grab her attention."

Brie pulled off the silver bow. and set it aside

as she tore at the pretty paper of the box she had carefully wrapped.

"Oh, Hope, look at all these fun books to read!" Brie had bought her a set of soft cloth books, each with a different animal on the cover. The books had peek-a-boo flaps and a variety of sounds and touch-and-feel textures for Hope to interact with. She held up the one with the cat on it. "What do you think?"

Hope took it from Brie and shook it several times before dropping it and reaching for the silver bow. Brie laughed and handed it to her.

"I think we could have bought a bunch of bows and she would have been just as happy."

Sir winked at her before getting up and leaving the room for a moment. When he returned, he had the bag of the extra bows. He let them fall all around Hope, and he was immediately rewarded with her squeals of laughter.

Hope let go of the silver one and grabbed a green one, trying to give it to Shadow.

Brie looked up at Sir, giggling.

"Apparently, our daughter has simple tastes, like her mother," Sir said with amusement.

Brie shrugged. "What can I say? I know what I want and I don't need anything else."

Sir sat down on the floor beside her. "And it's something I greatly admire about you, Brie."

"Sir, I actually made you something. I hope you like it."

He took her hands in his and said, "Anything made by these lovely hands will be perfect."

She smiled self-consciously as she grabbed the box wrapped in gold paper from under the tree and gave it to him. Brie watched with anticipation as he carefully unwrapped it and lifted the lid of the box.

"Interesting," he commented, taking out a digital frame.

"Press the button on the side," she instructed excitedly.

Sir moved closer to her so Hope could see the screen before he pressed the button.

"Arms Wide Open" by Creed began to play as photos of Sir and Hope flashed across the screen, starting from her delivery day to now.

Hope stared at it, transfixed, until the very end.

Sir watched it intently, saying nothing.

Afterward, Brie apologized. "I know the song says 'he' but—"

Sir stopped her, his voice choked with emotion. "Don't apologize. This…" He looked back at the screen that ended with of picture of him cradling Hope as she gazed up at him with a look of wonder. "The song and these pictures describe my feelings perfectly."

Brie smiled, wrapping her arms around him. "You are an amazing father, Thane Davis."

He put an arm around her as he reached out to caress Hope. "Thank you for giving me the chance to become one."

Sir grinned at Hope as he tossed several bows in the air. Shadow suddenly took an interest and started batting the bows across the floor like a kitten—much to the delight of their daughter.

"I love Christmas," Brie sighed in contentment, leaning against his shoulder.

Sir pulled out a small box from his pocket. "Even though you are a woman of simple tastes, I thought you might enjoy this."

Brie looked at him in surprise as she took the small red velvet box and opened it. Her heart skipped a beat when she saw it. She took out an elegant but simple gold bracelet engraved with the words "Condors Forever".

"I love it," she whispered, overcome with love.

Sir took it from her and fastened it around her wrist. Taking her hand, he kissed it tenderly. "You gave me a new life and I will always be indebted to you for it."

She shook her head, blushing. "I believe it was the other way around."

He kissed her passionately on the lips, murmuring, "I love you, Brie."

She returned his kisses, her heart bursting with joy.

"I love you, Thane."

Russian Gifts

At exactly one in the afternoon, per Rytsar's instructions, Brie, Sir, and Hope headed over to his house.

Brie couldn't wait for Rytsar to open his gift!

"I know he said he was keeping things simple this year, but I suspect Hope is exempt," she told Sir. "I have a feeling his tree will be overflowing with presents."

"I certainly hope not," Sir stated, ringing his doorbell.

Rytsar answered the door himself and spread his arms wide. "Merry Christmas!"

Hope reached out for Rytsar and he took her from Sir's arms. "Was Santa good to you, *moye solntse?*"

"Santa was," Brie giggled, "but all she was

interested in were the bows."

Rytsar laughed, smiling at Hope. "A young lady who knows what she wants." He looked at them, his eyes sparkling as he moved aside. "Come in, come in…"

Brie's attention immediately went to the tree, where she was surprised to see only one wrapped box. Maybe he really was going simple this year. The only problem was that his gift didn't have a bow. No matter how awesome the gift, Brie was unsure that Hope would care for it without a bow attached.

"I see you have a gift for me. Can I open it?" Rytsar asked, looking at the gift Brie held in her hand.

"Of course you can." She handed him the gift she had lovingly wrapped. "Merry Christmas!"

Rytsar took it from her and carried Hope to the couch with his faithful dog, Little Sparrow, sitting next to him. Setting Hope on his lap so he could unwrap the gift, he pulled off the red bow and handed it to her, making her giggle in delight.

"She'll be happy for the rest of the afternoon," Sir chuckled.

Rytsar ripped the paper, then suddenly stopped, tears coming to his eyes as he stared down at it.

Brie explained. "I remembered so vividly that moment when you returned to us and you hummed the lullaby to Hope and she smiled up at you. It was so beautiful. Inspired by your painting of your mother, I asked a local artist to capture that moment for me."

A single tear ran down his cheek as he finished unwrapping it and held it up for Hope to see. The charcoal drawing showed Hope cradled in Rytsar's arms. She was looking up at him with a big smile. His eyes sparkled with joy as he looked down at her. The artist had been able to capture the joy of that moment perfectly.

Rytsar looked at Brie and nodded, wiping the tear away.

She smiled at him lovingly. "Merry Christmas, Rytsar."

"Thank you, *radost moya*."

Brie felt that warm feeling she always associated with Christmas when she gave the perfect gift to someone she loved—there was nothing else like it.

Patting Little Sparrow's head, Rytsar asked

Sir, "Do you have anything for me?"

"I do, but it isn't time yet."

"Oh, being mysterious about it? I like that *moy droog*."

Rytsar gestured toward the tree. "*Radost moya*, would you get that present for me?"

"Of course." Brie walked to the ridiculously large Christmas tree. Rytsar had covered it in beautiful ornaments from Russia. She smiled when she noticed the little sun ornaments scattered throughout.

Bending down to get the gift, she heard a long wolf whistle. "Nice ass, wife."

Brie turned around and grinned at Sir. "Why thank you, husband."

She brought the gift, wrapped simply in brown paper, to Rytsar and sat down next to him to watch as he opened it for Hope.

Naturally, Hope was playing with the red bow and showed no interest as he unwrapped the gift.

"Don't take it personally," Brie told Rytsar.

"I'm not worried," he assured her. "I know exactly what this little girl needs."

He opened the box and pulled out a red leather bridle. "*Moye solntse*, this is for you!"

When he shook it, the metal made a tinkling sound that drew her attention for two seconds before she went back to playing with her bow.

Rytsar smiled as he called out to his man, Maxim. "Bring *moye solntse's* present to the front."

Maxim nodded and headed out the front door.

Sir stared at Rytsar. "You didn't."

"I did." Rytsar stood up, grinning as he headed out with Hope.

Brie and Sir followed behind him, looking at each other in surprise.

"She's much too young," Sir protested.

"Nonsense!" Rytsar declared as he walked through the front door with Hope just as Maxim rounded the corner, leading a beautiful white pony with a braided mane decorated with holly.

"A pony?" Brie cried.

"I call him *Malen'kiy Voin*, Little Berserker. But, naturally, *moye solntse* can call him whatever she likes."

"You are not giving her a pony," Sir stated.

"I already did," Rytsar said, smirking when Hope dropped her bow and bounced in Rytsar's arms, grasping for the pony.

He walked over to the animal and knelt down

so she could pet his white fur.

The pony turned his head and nickered softly.

Rytsar told them, "You have that area out back. I see no reason why you can't replace the hot tub with a pony-sized stable."

"You've got to be kidding," Sir said harshly.

Rytsar stood up and smiled at him. "I am!"

Sir frowned. "What?"

"*Moye solntse* is too little for a pony." He burst out laughing. "The look on your face, *moy droog*! Priceless."

Brie giggled, having bought it hook, line, and sinker. "You are wicked, Rytsar."

Rytsar knelt back down so Hope could pet the pony again, saying, "I borrowed him from a friend. You do not have to worry about losing your precious hot tub, comrade."

"That was never going to happen," Sir asserted.

"Bring the pony inside," Rytsar told Maxim as he headed back into the house.

"You're bringing him inside?" Brie laughed.

"Of course," Rytsar stated as if it were a normal thing to do.

When Brie walked into the house, her jaw

dropped. The tree which had been empty of presents before was now full of them, and Little Sparrow lay with her tail wagging as she chewed on a ridiculously large bone.

"You claimed you were going simple this year," Sir stated when he saw the mound of presents.

Rytsar shrugged. "Eh? What's the point of having money if you can't spend it on the people you love?"

"So that was all an act?" Brie laughed.

"*Da.* I am not a man to hold back."

"You never were," Sir muttered.

Rytsar showered Hope in bows as he unwrapped the multitude of gifts he'd bought for her. But the one that touched Brie's heart the most was the vintage pull toy of a Russian circus horse.

Rytsar opened it and told Hope. "When I was a little boy, I had one just like this. It was my favorite toy."

After he was done showing it to Hope, Brie asked, "Can I see it?"

When Rytsar handed it to her, she noticed a special glint in his eyes and knew it brought back good memories for him.

Brie looked at the prancing white horse on a blue stand with wheels underneath. The toy had a braided cord with a blue wooden ball for a child to grasp as they pulled it across the floor.

The old toy was charming and like nothing she'd had growing up. Brie could imagine Rytsar as a tiny boy pulling his own toy horse. The image brought her great joy.

It wasn't lost on Brie that both Rytsar's horse *Voin*, and the little pony he'd brought today bore a striking resemblance to the toy.

"I think I need a break from all this chaos, and I bet the pony does, too," Sir stated, looking at the mountain of wrapping paper and boxes scattered about.

"Excellent idea," Rytsar agreed. "Let's breathe in the ocean."

Rytsar picked up Hope and handed her a gold bow. Meanwhile, Maxim snapped on the lead rope to the pony's bridle and then handed it to Rytsar.

They walked outside, heading to the water with the pony following behind them.

As they stood there, watching the waves come in, Brie heard a single-engine plane above them and looked up. "Oh my!"

The other two looked up as the plane finished writing first a number sign followed by the number one.

Brie grinned. "Isn't that sweet? I loved when you did that for Hope, Rytsar."

The Russian smiled, shielding his eyes from the sun as he looked up at the plane. "'#1' at what, though?" he asked.

The three of them watched the plane swing around to make the letter "D".

"Dad," Rytsar stated. "It must be 'Dad.'"

Sir nudged Brie. "Is this your doing, babygirl?"

She shook her head, blushing. "I'm sorry, Sir, but I wish I'd thought of it."

Brie looked back up, anxious to see what the next letter was.

When the plane made the letter "Y", Rytsar chuckled. "Ah, so you did this for me, *radost moya*," he stated proudly.

Brie blushed a deeper shade of red. "Sorry, no."

"Don't be such a narcissist, Durov," Sir admonished. "It's obvious he's spelling out the word 'dynamo.' It's the only other word that makes sense."

They all watched to see if he was right, but the next letter was definitely an "A".

When it swung back around and made another "D" there was no mistaking the word.

"*'Dyadya'*. I knew it!" Rytsar shouted, grinning wide. "Confess. Which one of you did this?"

Brie laughed. "It wasn't me."

They both looked at Sir, who shrugged modestly.

Rytsar chuckled as he handed Hope to Brie. Walking over to Sir, Rytsar embraced him in a bear hug. "You are trickier than you look, *moy droog*."

Sir returned the hug, laughing.

While Rytsar looked back up at the sky, Sir got his phone out and started recording.

"I can't believe you called me a narcissist when I was right," Rytsar complained.

"Well, you are," Sir answered, grinning as he continued to record the skywriting.

Rytsar said nothing for several moments while the plane finished the message and then said, "Thank you for this, brother. It means more than I can say."

Sir turned to look at him, his phone still focused on the sky. "I thought you'd like it."

Looking back up at the message in the sky," Sir added, "I speak only the truth, brother."

Tears came to Brie's eyes, deeply moved by the love Sir and Rytsar had for each other.

When the plane flew off and the letters were only wisps in the air, the four of them, along with the pony, headed back to his house.

"I want to show you something in my garage," Rytsar stated. He handed Maxim the pony's lead and ordered him to open the garage.

As the garage door slowly rose, Rytsar stated, "I have always wanted to own one of these…"

Inside was a classic, black Harley Davidson with chrome pipes.

"Oh, Rytsar, it's beautiful!" Brie cried walking up to the motorcycle and running Hope's tiny hand over the studded black leather seat. "Doesn't your *dyadya* have a pretty bike?"

Rytsar winked at Brie. "I'm glad you like it, *radost moya*."

Sir studied the bike for a moment and then turned to face Rytsar. "Those gloves you got me…"

The Russian's smile grew wider.

"They're motorcycle gloves, aren't they?"

"They are, *moy droog*."

Sir looked back at the bike. "And this?"

"Is your present," he proclaimed, slapping Sir hard on the back. "Merry Christmas!"

Shaking his head, Sir looked back at the motorcycle. "It's a beauty, but I don't know how to ride one."

"Sit on the bike," Rytsar insisted.

Sir gave him a half-grin as he mounted it and grabbed the handles.

"You look like a natural, *moy droog*."

"I have to agree, Sir," Brie said, getting all kinds of sexy vibes seeing him on the bike.

"Look how your woman approves," Rytsar stated proudly.

"I can't accept this. It's too much," Sir told him.

"Wait here," Rytsar insisted.

As he headed into the house, Sir got off the bike and stood back to admire it. "I have to say he's got good taste."

"You really do look hot on that bike," Brie confessed.

He chuckled. "Thanks, but I'm not going to let him give this to me. It's *way* too much for a Christmas present." Sir stood back, staring at the bike, and muttered, "What the hell was he thinking?"

Just then, the air filled with the deep rumbling of a motorcycle.

Brie squeaked when she saw Rytsar pull into the driveway on a candy apple red Harley that looked just like Sir's.

Rytsar revved the engine once before shutting it off and getting off the bike. "I liked yours so much that I got one, too, brother."

Sir laughed. "You're impossible."

"Just imagine the two of us on the road, your woman seated behind with her arms around you as we explore the country together."

"It does sound enticing, but I still can't accept it."

"Why not?" Rytsar frowned.

"It's too much."

"It would not be nearly as much fun for me to ride alone," Rytsar stated. "This gift is as much for me as it is for you."

Sir snorted.

Changing tactics, Rytsar turned to Brie. "Wouldn't you like to ride with your Master on this bike, *radost moya*?"

Even though Brie knew the answer Sir wanted her to give, she told Rytsar the truth. "That would be so hot!"

Rytsar shrugged, telling Sir, "Do you really want to disappoint your woman, *moy droog*?"

Sir shook his head. "The lengths you will go to…"

Rytsar dug into his pocket and pulled out the set of keys. "Accept my gift in the spirit it is given."

Sir stared at the keys for a second before taking them.

Rytsar grinned. "I have a private lesson set up for you in two days' time."

"Why so soon?" Sir laughed.

Rytsar glanced at Brie with a seductive smile. "Because I'm going to give *radost moya* her gift during your first ride."

Brie smiled, her mind racing as she tried to figure out what it might be.

A Gathering

After their visit with Rytsar, Brie and Sir went back home to put Hope down for a nap.

"This is the best Christmas I've ever had, Sir. Between your morning presents to me and the gifts you and Rytsar gave each other, I can't think of a more perfect day.

Sir wrapped an arm around her. "I agree, babygirl. Despite the memories the holiday evokes, I have enjoyed myself, and it has everything to do with you."

Brie sighed in contentment. "Now to start on dinner. I want to spoil you, Sir. I bought everything for a traditional Christmas dinner."

Sir smiled. "Is the turkey defrosted?"

She frowned. "No. I didn't think to do that."

"Don't worry about it. I'm not into all that holiday fare. A simple salad will suffice."

Her jaw dropped. "We can't eat a plain old salad on Christmas day! Maybe I could order a turkey dinner?"

"They would have been sold out weeks ago."

She was completely crushed. "But I wanted to spoil you, Sir. Especially after everything you've done for me."

He shrugged. "It really doesn't matter."

She pouted. "It does to me!"

"There's only one thing I want to eat for Christmas."

Brie blushed, grinning at him. "You can't live on pussy alone, Sir."

"Watch me."

She broke out in giggles.

Sir looked down at his watch. "And, right now, I'm in the mood for an afternoon snack."

When he held out his hand to her, Brie took it eagerly.

He led her to his secret playroom, calling out the secret code that opened the door.

Sweeping her up into his arms, Sir carried her into the playroom and placed her on the binding table.

He stripped off her panties, then buckled the leather cuffs around her wrists and smiled lustfully as he spread her legs wide. With a glint in his eye, he left her for a moment. When Sir returned, he was wearing the motorcycle gloves that Rytsar had given him.

"Don't move," he commanded in a tone that made her insides quiver as he ran his hand over her pussy.

He continued to pet her, the feel of the leather adding a friction she hadn't experienced before, and she liked it—a lot.

"I have always found your pussy exquisite. That inviting mound..." He ran his gloved hand over it. "The soft folds..." His fingers traced them lightly. "Your wet inner lips..." He spread them apart. "And that sensitive clit that begs for my attention..." Sir rubbed it slowly, teasing her.

"All of it inviting me to taste, lick, and suck."

Sir settled down between her legs and smiled at her as he took a slow, long lick.

Brie whimpered, loving the feel of his tongue on her clit.

Spreading her legs wider, he teased her with his tongue and soon had Brie moaning with glorious need. Because of her bound wrists, she was forced to lay there and simply enjoy his talented mouth.

When he began licking and sucking with greater intensity, her thighs started to quiver. She was so close…

Brie heard the doorbell ring and froze. "Do we pretend we're not home, Master?"

Sir looked up from between her legs.

Her heart stopped when she heard the pounding on the door and her father's voice. "Brianna, don't leave us standing here. We've come a long way."

"It's my dad!" she cried in panic.

Sir stood up slowly, wiping his mouth before he unbound her wrists. "Slip on your panties, lock this door, freshen up, and join me," he commanded calmly as he took off the gloves and laid them on the table.

Brie jumped down from the table, struggling to get her panties on in her harried state. She heard Sir answer the door and her parents' voices as he invited them in.

What are my parents doing here?

She called out the code and the door slowly closed. She then ran to reapply her makeup and brush out her hair while her poor pussy continued to throb with need.

Taking a deep breath, she opened the bedroom door and walked out. "Mom! Dad!"

"About time you came out to greet us," her father scolded.

"Brie was up early this morning and I suggested she take a nap," Sir explained.

Her father opened his arms to her. "Well, my tuckered little girl, come to Daddy." Brie grinned as she walked up and he enfolded her in his arms. "Merry Christmas."

"Merry Christmas, Daddy."

Brie turned to her mother next. "This is such a wonderful surprise!"

"Thane wanted you to have your family here for Christmas."

Brie glanced over at Sir. "You knew they were coming?"

"I invited them and got the text when they landed." He smirked, subtly wiping his mouth. "But I was hoping for a little more time…so you could rest."

Brie blushed.

"Are you feeling okay, sweetheart?" her mother asked with concern.

She smiled reassuringly. "I have never felt

better, Mom, and look…" She pointed to the nativity set on the coffee table.

"Aww!" Her mother walked over to it. "It looks just perfect there." She turned back to face Brie with tears in her eyes. "I'm so happy."

"Don't start, Marcy," her father ordered.

"She's been a sentimental mess this year," he explained to Sir.

"No harm in that," Sir replied, smiling at Brie's mom.

"So, where's my granddaughter, Brianna?" her father demanded.

"Sorry, Daddy. We just put her down for a nap. She won't be up for another hour at least."

"Just enough time to get everything started for dinner," her mother announced.

Brie frowned. "Unfortunately, I forgot to defrost the turkey. We won't be having much I'm afraid."

"Not to worry, babygirl," Sir assured her. "Unc has been up since five cooking a turkey."

"They're coming over, too?"

"I knew you wanted to have a holiday meal with family."

Brie ran to him, hugged him tightly. "It will be wonderful to have a full table for Christmas."

The doorbell rang again.

Brie looked back at Sir excitedly as she walked over to open it and cried out in surprise. "Lea!"

Giggling immediately followed.

Lea handed her a bowl.

"What's this?"

"Green bean casserole. It's not Christmas without it."

Brie carried the bowl into the kitchen, telling her mom, "Look what Lea brought. That's one less thing we have to make."

Soon after, the doorbell rang again. Brie didn't have to guess who it was because Rytsar yelled, "Let me in, *radost moya*."

Running to the door, she flung it open to see Rytsar carrying a large basket.

"What's this?" she asked smelling fresh-baked bread when he handed it to her.

"Maxim and I tried our hand at my mother's piroshkis." He looked back at Maxim, who was holding several gifts in his hands. "We did her proud, didn't we?"

Maxim nodded.

"I can't wait to try them!" Brie exclaimed, inviting them both in.

Brie watched with joy as Rytsar took one of the gifts Maxim was holding and gave it to her father.

Her father actually smiled.

True to his word, Rytsar was slowly winning his way into her father's heart, like the good *dyadya* he was.

When the doorbell rang again, Brie heard Hope start to cry.

"I'll get her," Brie's mother insisted as she headed up the stairs.

Brie opened the door and let out a surprised gasp. "Tono and Autumn!"

Tono's smile warmed her heart. "Merry Christmas, Mrs. Davis."

Brie grabbed both their hands and pulled them inside. "I'm so happy to see you. This is such a wonderful surprise."

"Since I can't be with my own family this Christmas, there is no other place I would rather be," Autumn told her as she handed Brie a platter.

"And, what did you bring?" Brie asked, curious about her dish.

Autumn grinned. "Tono and I made gyoza. We can pan fry them for an appetizer or with the meal."

"I'll put them in the fridge for the meal. How does that sound?"

"Perfect."

Brie walked them over to her parents, who were busy fawning over Hope.

It felt wonderful to have a full house at Christmas. Brie looked at Sir, touched that he'd done this for her.

Apparently, it was about to get a little fuller because she heard the doorbell again.

Expecting Sir's aunt and uncle, Brie was shocked to see Ms. Clark. "Merry Christmas, Ms. Clark."

She nodded curtly. "Happy holidays, Mrs. Davis."

Brie was a little surprised that Sir had invited the Domme but greeted her warmly. "Won't you please come in?"

"I've brought the required addition to the meal," she said, handing Brie a heavy dish. "I hope you like ham."

"Christmas isn't Christmas without it," Brie declared. "Let me put this in the oven to keep warm and I'll introduce you to my parents."

As Brie put the dish in the kitchen, she

watched Rytsar's reaction when Ms. Clark entered the room. He stared at the Domme and gave her a friendly nod when their eyes met.

Glancing at Sir, Brie saw that he was observing them, as well. However, he wore a relaxed expression. She assumed he must have spoken to Rytsar about it beforehand.

When the doorbell rang again, Brie hurried to the door wanting to give the Reynolds a big hug. Instead, she found Mary standing all alone with a dish in her hands.

"Wow, Mary, I sure didn't expect to see you. Come in, come in!"

As she passed by Brie, Mary said, "Greg is socializing with all of his business associates today. I couldn't stomach it and thought I would take Sir Davis up on his offer for a meal."

"Well, I'm happy you did," Brie said, giving her a hard squeeze.

Mary handed off her dish to Brie, saying, "I brought toasted Brie. I thought it was fitting after our Kinky Eve event."

"I love this!"

Brie grinned as she headed to the kitchen to show her mother Mary's dish.

"What a wonderful group of friends you

have," her mom said, looking at the house crowded with people.

"I really do, Mom."

"When I think of you coming to LA on your own and working at that little tobacco shop to make ends meet while you took your college classes, it's amazing to see how far you've come."

Brie glanced at Sir, who was talking with Autumn and Tono. "It's all because of him."

"No, honey. It's because you never let anything stop you." She put her hands on Brie's cheeks. "I'm so proud of you, my dear, sweet daughter. You've exceeded everything I ever hoped for you."

Brie smiled, looking at her mother tenderly. "You gave me the foundation to do it."

"And you ran with it. Boy, did you run with it." She kissed Brie on the cheek and then fussed, "I'd better get to peeling more potatoes. You've got a full house here."

Lea offered to help Brie set the table. "Wow, this is amazing, girlfriend. I was dreading spending Christmas alone because my parents headed off to New York to spend the holidays with my dad's family."

"I'm so tickled I get to share Christmas with you."

Looking at the gathering, Lea said, "I'm surprised Master Anderson isn't here. Is he running late?"

Brie answered her as she set the forks and knives. "Since Shey isn't here, I heard his family flew down to spend Christmas with him."

"It's so sweet of them to do that."

"Isn't it? I haven't met his family yet, but I hope to while they're here."

When the doorbell rang again, Sir held out his hand to Brie. Together, they answered the door.

"Merry Christmas!" Brie cried when she saw the Reynolds.

"We're happy you made it safely, Unc," Sir said, taking the giant foiled pan from him.

"Handle that with care, Thane. I put a lot of love into that turkey."

"Will do, Unc."

Mr. Reynolds went back to their van to get baby Jonathan.

"Brie, can you help me with these pies?"

Brie laughed as she took the giant container from Judy. "How many pies do you have in here?"

"I wasn't sure what everyone wanted so I made pumpkin, apple, pecan, and cherry."

"You definitely covered all the bases." Brie grinned.

"You can never have too much pie!" Judy exclaimed. "Now, I have to run back to the car to get the stuffing and gravy, as well as all the fixings for the pies."

Brie called out, "I'll meet you by the refrigerator."

Returning to the kitchen, Brie was amazed at how efficiently her mother was running it. With such a large space, there was plenty of room for everyone to prepare for the meal.

"I love this kitchen, honey," her mom told her. "It's so elegant and spacious."

"Isn't it perfect for the holidays?" Brie said, smiling with contentment.

Sir's uncle, Jack, called out to everyone. "Come see this magnificent bird before we start carving it."

Everyone gathered to watch, admiring the perfect golden brown color he'd gotten on the turkey. Jack held up the knife to give to Sir. "Would you like to do the honors?"

Sir waved his hand. "No, Unc. The honor should be yours. You're the one who got up at the crack of dawn to cook it."

"Very well," his uncle said with a smile, winking at Brie.

While Mr. Reynolds entertained the crowd with his carving skills, Brie helped carry all the food to the table. With twelve guests for dinner, the table was overflowing with food, just the way Brie had always imagined it.

"Please, come sit," she called to everyone. "Dinner is ready."

Sir sat at the head of the table with Brie to his left. Rytsar insisted on holding Hope during the meal and sat beside Brie. Her parents sat next to Rytsar with Sir's aunt and uncle sitting across from Brie with Jonathan in between them in Hope's highchair. Tono and Autumn sat beside them with Lea at the far end next to Ms. Clark. Ms. Clark chose to sit at the opposite end from Sir with Mary beside on her left.

A full table in every sense of the word.

"Oh, wait," Brie said, popping out of her seat. She hurried to the kitchen and hit play, setting Alonzo's Christmas album at a low level. She wanted him to be a part of their first

Christmas meal together as a family.

Sir nodded to her as she sat down.

Addressing their guests, Sir said, "We want to thank you for being here with us today. Each of you has played a significant role in our lives and we are grateful to share this day and meal with you."

Smiling at Jack, Sir informed them, "I have asked my uncle to say a blessing before we begin."

Sir sat down and took Brie's hand. Alonzo's violin played softly in the background as everyone joined hands. Bowing her head, Brie listened as Mr. Reynolds prayed.

"Heavenly Father, we ask that you bless this bounty before us and the people gathered here. We are honored to celebrate with Thane, Brie, and Hope on this special day. May the bonds between us grow stronger with every Christmas that passes and may the joy of the season remain in our hearts all through the year. In the name of Jesus Christ, Amen."

Brie smiled as she repeated, "Amen." She looked over at Sir, her heart full of love.

"Let's eat!" Rytsar declared.

People chuckled before digging in, filling

their plates with the wonderful food everyone had brought.

Rytsar cut a pickle in half and asked Brie, "Shall we see what *moye solntse* thinks of my favorite food?"

"Let's!"

Brie watched with amusement as he brought the dill pickle to Hope's lips. She opened her mouth hungrily but when she bit down, she got a shocked look on her face and pulled away, crinkling her face as she shuddered.

Everyone laughed.

"Is it too sour for you, Hope?" Brie's father asked her.

In answer, Hope opened her mouth and eagerly took another taste, exhibiting the exact same reaction.

"*Moye solntse* likes it," Rytsar declared proudly, kissing the top of her head.

Brie took Sir's hand under the table and squeezed it. This was everything she had hoped for and more. She struggled not to get teary as she watched her friends and family talking and laughing at their table.

And then Rytsar did something truly extraordinary.

Near the end of the meal, the mood in the room had become relaxed and intimate. After taking a shot of vodka, Rytsar handed Hope to Brie and turned his attention on Ms. Clark. "I have something to say…"

The room fell silent as everyone's gaze landed on him.

"You have been living a lie."

Rolling her shoulders back and steeling herself for his wrath, she said, "Okay."

"Samantha, you are not the same woman you were sixteen years ago. You are not your scars—or mine. Stop living in the past. I command it."

He stood up from the table.

"You have the power to embrace the person you've fought so hard to become. You are enough, Samantha, right now. Own it."

Brie felt chills on hearing his pronouncement.

Ms. Clark stared at him, saying nothing, her breath coming in rapid gasps.

"Agreed," Sir said, looking directly at her.

The silence in the room grew more profound as the power behind Rytsar's words sank in.

Finally, Ms. Clark bowed her head slightly. "Thank you, Anton."

Rytsar nodded and sat down.

Everyone stared at Rytsar in stunned silence.

Uncomfortable with the attention, he took Hope back from Brie and declared, "Make merry!"

But Brie couldn't take her eyes off him.

Of all the gifts that had been given today, his was the most selfless and powerful.

Rumble in the Hills

After Sir had successfully completed his motorcycle class, he asked Brie to join him on his first bike ride with Rytsar through the hills just outside LA. With Brie's parents staying at their house for the remainder of the holidays, it left her free to join him.

"You better drive safe," her father warned Sir. "You not only have my only daughter on the back of that motorbike but the young mother of my granddaughter. I don't want anything happening to her. You hear me?"

"Dad—" Brie started to protest, but Sir stopped her.

"I assure you that I will be vigilant. My entire life is invested in my wife."

Sir's answer seemed to appease her father,

but Brie could see the concern in her mother's eyes.

"Don't worry, Mom," Brie assured her. "Sir is an excellent driver and Rytsar will be with us during the entire ride."

"It's just...motorcycles," she whimpered, looking at the bike as if it was a dangerous weapon.

Brie chuckled. "It's going to be fine, Mom and, when I get back, I'll tell you all about it."

Her mother squeezed Hope closer to her. "Just be safe, sweetheart."

Brie kissed her cheek and gave Hope a tender kiss on the forehead. "We will."

Equipped with a helmet, leather jacket, and pants, Brie felt fully protected as she climbed onto Sir's sexy Harley and sat behind him.

When he turned the engine on, Brie purred in delight. There was something erotically primal about that deep rumble from the bike as she wrapped her arms around Sir and pressed her body against him.

Sir headed out, driving down to Rytsar's house, where they found he was already waiting for them. As soon as they drew close, he revved his engine several times.

Brie grinned, loving the sound of the bike. When she waved at him, he nodded to her and pointed to a big box strapped to his bike. It had to be her belated Christmas present.

She couldn't wait to open it!

Sir led the way as they headed out together. Brie couldn't stop smiling, so enchanted by the power of the bike and the freedom it offered.

She could feel the wind against her face and smell the flowers as they passed by the pink jasmine bushes on the way to the highway.

Once they merged onto the 105, Sir took off. Brie squealed with excitement, holding on tight as he matched the speed of the cars.

Rytsar pulled up beside Sir and they rode side by side.

It was a girl's orgasmic dream to be on the bike as she headed toward the hills, accompanied by these two men.

Something that Brie hadn't expected was that other bikers waved to them as they passed. She felt as if she had been adopted into a whole new community, and she loved it.

As they headed into the hills, Brie moved in tandem with Sir, leaning as he leaned. It connected her to him even more as they experienced the road together.

Sir veered off the main highway, taking an abandoned road. He had to slow way down to navigate the bumpy terrain.

When Sir finally reached his destination, he parked the bike off the road and helped her off it before dismounting himself.

He took off his helmet and gloves and then swiped his fingers through his hair.

Hot damn, he was sexy!

Brie unbuttoned her jacket and laid it on the bike, setting her helmet on top of it.

"What do you think, *moy droog*?" Rytsar asked, walking up to them with a huge grin on his face.

"I should have gotten a motorcycle a long time ago."

Rytsar chuckled. "*Da!*"

He turned his attention on Brie. "And, you…you look mighty fine on a bike, *radost moya*."

"I absolutely love the feeling of it."

"I know what you would love even more…" He gestured to the box on his bike.

"Can I open it now?"

"Of course." Rytsar walked over with her and undid the straps, handing it to her. "Merry

Christmas, *radost moya*."

Brie lifted the lid and sifted through the mountains of tissue paper. Inside, she found an alluring black leather bikini, six-inch candy apple red heels, and a tube of bright red lipstick.

"These are sexy, Rytsar," she told him.

He winked at her and asked Sir, "Did you bring your camera, *moy droog*?"

"I did."

Rytsar looked at Brie lustfully. "I want to do a photo shoot with you draped over my bike."

Sir gave Brie a small, insulated backpack and winked at her. "Some wine and cheese while we wait for the bikes to cool down."

"How fun is this!"

Brie picked an area in the shade and they sat down together, taking in the view of LA while she sipped the red wine and nibbled on the cheese.

After a long silence, Rytsar said, "I never thought life could be this peaceful."

"It's been a long time coming, old friend."

Rytsar nodded. "It has, *moy droog*."

Turning to Brie, he asked, "What are your plans this coming year?"

"I'm planning to get my documentary released, but I was thinking of filming one more scene before I show it to the producer."

"Really?"

"Yes, Master Nosh agreed to an interview. I think he would add an interesting perspective to the film being a trainer of Dominants."

"It would definitely add a new element. I look forward to seeing it." Rytsar threw back the rest of his wine before getting up to check on his bike.

Brie looked at Sir. She was trying to build up the courage to address something that had been on her mind since the charity event. "Sir, do you remember when I told you I wanted to donate a million dollars to the recovery center in your name?"

He chuckled. "I do. I have to admit that I was flattered even though you were obviously giddy from your sub high."

"I'm amazed at how much money the event raised, and I'm grateful we donated as much money as we did to Tatianna's center."

Brie saw the pain in his eyes when he told her, "How could we not give generously after what almost happened to you and Hope? I almost lost you both…"

Brie knew Sir still struggled with guilt over the attempted kidnapping. She moved closer to him, placing her hand on his cheek as she gazed into his eyes. "We were spared that tragedy. Because of that, I feel more determined than ever to help those who have not been as lucky as we were." She paused for a moment. "I would like to add significantly to our donation with my next documentary."

Sir looked at her questioningly. "What exactly do you mean, babygirl?"

"I want to donate the money I make on the newest film to the Tatianna Legacy Center."

His gaze didn't leave hers. When he said nothing, she added, "Of course, it's a decision we both have to agree on."

"Whatever you make from the documentary would add to our income, but it is not a necessity. If that is how you wish to use the money, I would fully support you in that."

Brie felt relief flow through her. "It means so much that you understand."

Sir wrapped his arms around her. "Every day I wake up and breathe a sigh of relief that you and Hope are safe. I will be grateful for that for as long as I live."

Brie nodded with tears in her eyes, returning his hug.

"You may want to mention your plans to Mary," he suggested. "She may be able to convince Holloway to donate some of his earnings, as well."

Brie's eyes lit up and she hugged him tighter. "That's brilliant, Sir."

"What are you two talking about so seriously?" Rytsar asked, walking back to them.

Wanting it to be a surprise, Brie told him, "I'm considering different options for the film."

Rytsar grinned. "I'm looking forward to being there for the world premiere."

Brie felt a thrill of excitement as she thought about the future of her documentary. With such a powerful film to offer and money to be raised, there was a chance to make a real difference in the world.

"My bike is ready for you to ride her," Rytsar informed Brie with a wicked grin, handing her the box.

"Great. Where should I change?"

"Right here in front of me."

Brie giggled nervously and then looked at Sir, who nodded his approval.

Taking command of the moment, Brie offered them a sexy striptease as she undressed and donned the skimpy leather bikini. Slipping into the red heels and putting on the lipstick, she stood in place as she spun around. "How do I look?"

"Edible," Sir answered.

"Come with me." Rytsar stared at her hungrily as he took her hand and helped her walk in her heels over the uneven terrain to the bike.

Sir got his camera out of the storage compartment of his bike and took his position, adjusting the camera while Rytsar directed her first pose.

"Crouch at the back of the bike and sit on your heels with your legs spread."

Putting her hand on the motorcycle for balance, she took the pose.

"Open your legs a little wider, babygirl. Back straight. Keep your left hand on the bike and put your right hand on your thigh," Sir instructed.

"Oh, that's it. Very sexy, *radost moya*," Rytsar complimented.

After taking several shots, Rytsar moved on to the next pose.

"Sit on my bike. Put your left hand on the

handle and twist your waist, putting your right hand behind you."

Brie felt like a real model as she took the position and heard him grunt in approval.

"Babygirl, move your leg forward. I want your knee higher."

"Like this?"

"Perfect."

When Sir was finished taking pictures of the pose, Rytsar told her, "Now, lie down on your back with your body lying on the tank and your sexy ass on the seat."

Brie turned around and lay against the warm tank, careful not to let the heels of her shoes scratch his new bike.

"Arch your back, babygirl."

Brie arched her back more while Rytsar adjusted the position of her legs. "Hold it right there," he commanded.

After he backed away, Sir ordered her to arch her back even more. All of her muscles began to shake as she tried to hold the pose.

Rytsar let out a long whistle of appreciation. "Damn, *radost moya*. You make my bike look fucking hot."

Brie smiled at him, then looked into the lens

of Sir's camera, thinking wicked thoughts, hoping they would translate to film.

She was grateful when Sir finally said he had gotten enough pictures and she could relax. Rytsar came over and took off her shoes, caressing her legs as he did so.

Brie purred in pleasure.

Rytsar then untied her bikini top and let it fall to the ground. Sir set his camera down and walked over to join them.

Both men stood to either side of the bike and descended on her breasts at the same time. Brie moaned passionately, her pussy wet with need as she looked up at the blue sky while they sucked, tugged and pinched her nipples.

Sir undid the ties of her bikini bottom and removed it, leaving her completely exposed to them. Both men sought out her pussy with their fingers, one rubbing her clit while the other penetrated her vagina to rub her G-spot. It didn't take long to reach the edge with their concentrated attention.

"Christen my bike with your orgasm," Rytsar demanded.

With permission given, Brie relaxed, not resisting the buildup as they teased her pussy to perfection. She felt a chill course through her just before her muscles tightened as they readied for release.

Keeping the same rhythm with their fingers, Rytsar and Sir took her over the edge. Forgetting where she was, Brie started to scream as she came but Sir covered her mouth with his, muting her cries.

Her entire body trembled from the intensity of it as she gushed with watery come.

"Good girl," Rytsar growled huskily.

Afterward, she lay on the bike moaning softly, weak from the powerful orgasm.

"I need you," Sir whispered, biting her bottom lip after kissing her.

Looking at Rytsar, he said, "I want us to take her at the same time."

Brie squeaked when Sir picked her up and held onto her as Rytsar unzipped his pants, freeing his hard shaft.

Lying on the bike, holding his rigid shaft in his hand, he beckoned to her.

Sir helped Brie straddle Rytsar as she slowly settled down on his cock.

Rytsar grabbed her waist, pushing her farther down. Brie growled lustfully, enjoying the fullness of his shaft.

Sir straddled the bike behind her, rubbing his cock against her ass cheeks, still wet from her watery come. He pressed the slippery head of his shaft against her tight opening.

"Are you ready, babygirl?" he growled lustfully.

Placing one hand over her mouth, he pushed his cock inside her. Brie screamed in pleasure, his hand muting her cries as he forced his cock deep in her ass.

Having already come, her body was desperate for more and opened itself to his manly invasion.

Both men began thrusting into her, moving as one as their shafts stimulated her G-spot mercilessly. It was impossible not to come and her body shuddered from the intensity of her second orgasm.

Sir and Rytsar groaned as her inner muscles squeezed their cocks rhythmically during her climax.

The thrill of having sex out in the open seemed to turn both men on. When Sir grabbed her hips and Rytsar clutched her waist, Brie knew she was in delicious trouble.

Brie closed her eyes as the two ramped it up,

fucking her so hard and deep that she struggled not to cry out. Her body started to tingle as another climax snuck up on her.

Rytsar's passionate grunts filled her ears as she came a third time. It sent Rytsar over the edge with her and he came deep in her pussy.

Sir continued to fuck her, ramming his cock repeatedly into her ass until he'd reached his limit and came himself.

The feeling of Sir releasing his seed deep in her ass was so erotic that her pussy started pulsing again and she came a fourth and final time.

Afterward, Rytsar pulled a jug of water out of his storage compartment and they each took a long drink before he poured the cool water over her hot pussy. Brie purred in pleasure, enjoying its soothing coolness.

As they dressed and got ready to head back home, Rytsar walked over and kissed Brie on the forehead. "There is another gift in the box."

Brie grinned as she removed all the tissue paper from it and found an envelope taped to the bottom. Pulling it off, Brie read the note he had written on the envelope.

Your gift is related to the flower.

Brie remembered the white flower on the silver toe ring he had given her and looked at him curiously. Opening the envelope, she saw an overhead shot of an island with the date of Dec 31st written across it.

"Is that the Isle?"

Rytsar nodded, a wicked glint in his eye.

Warm Afterglow

As the day ended, Brie settled on the couch to watch the colorful lights on the Christmas tree. She felt a little melancholy knowing that the holidays were coming to an end.

After checking on Hope, Sir joined her on the couch.

She curled up against him, smiling.

"How are you feeling, babygirl?"

Even knowing her parents were asleep in the guestroom, Brie answered truthfully, "My pussy is still delightfully sore from the bike ride."

He chuckled. "That's good to hear."

After several moments of comfortable silence, Brie murmured, "I love Christmas lights. They make me happy."

Sir began playing with her hair. She purred in

contentment as she watched the lights dance on the tree.

"I received a letter from my grandfather," he told her.

"Is everything okay?"

"Yes. However, he mentioned that Nonna has been asking to see us."

Brie lifted her head. "I would love to see them again."

"Good. I was considering stopping by Portoferraio for a few days after we visit the Isle."

"It would be wonderful for Nonno and Nonna to see how much Hope has grown, and it will make the holidays last a little longer for me."

Sir smiled. "My Nonna bakes up a storm for the holidays. I would love you to experience that."

"It sounds wonderful, Sir."

"Good, then. I will call him tomorrow and let the family know we're coming."

Sir went back to playing with her hair.

Brie sighed happily. "Best Christmas ever…"

He had a wistful look on his face when he said, "I haven't wanted to acknowledge Christmas since my father died, but you forced me to."

She looked at him sadly. "I never meant to

hurt you, Sir. I'm sorry if it has."

He shook his head, smiling slightly. "I needed to face it at some point. Having a child definitely gives the day more meaning and has made it easier for me." He let out a sigh. "Her innocent wonder helps heal a wounded heart."

"Yes," Brie agreed.

She glanced back at the Christmas tree and smiled. "You know, I never realized how fascinating bows were until Hope."

Sir chuckled. "She was cute today."

Brie kissed him on the cheek. "I want to thank you for everything you've done, Sir."

"What? Made you a cup of hot chocolate and called a few people over for dinner?"

Brie smiled, touched that he was being so modest by choosing not to mention the many things he'd done, including his involvement in spearheading Kinky Eve and the beautiful bracelet she now wore.

"You are a thoughtful Master, and you gave this little sub everything she could possibly desire."

He cupped her chin, turning her head so he could look into her eyes. "It is my pleasure, téa. You continually inspire me with your curiosity and devotion."

The love she felt for him was so overwhelming it almost hurt. "I love you, Master."

"I love you, téa."

Brie settled against him again, thoroughly content. She watched the tree in silence, the warm afterglow of Christmas filling her heart.

"So, you like this tree?"

"I do, Sir."

"I suppose having a tree next year isn't out of the question."

Brie smiled to herself.

"That would be lovely, Sir."

I hope you enjoyed *Hope's First Christmas!*
COMING UP NEXT—*Secrets of the Heart: Brie's Submission Book 20*

The next book in the Brie Series
March 2020!
Read the next book of Brie!
(Release Date – March 3, 2020)

~~~~~~~

** You can begin the journey of Sir, Rytsar and Master Anderson when they first met!**
Start reading Sir's Rise the 1st book in the Rise of the Dominants Trilogy

COMING NEXT

Secrets of the Heart:
Book 20 of Brie's Submission
Available for Preorder

Reviews mean the world to me!

I truly appreciate you taking the time to review ***Hope's First Christmas***.

If you could leave a review on both Goodreads and the site where you purchased this eBook from, I would be so grateful. Sincerely, ~Red

You can begin the journey of Sir, Rytsar and Master Anderson when they first met with *Sir's Rise* the 1st book in the *Rise of the Dominants Series*!

Start reading NOW!

ABOUT THE AUTHOR

Over Two Million readers have enjoyed Red's stories

Red Phoenix – USA Today Bestselling Author
Winner of 8 Readers' Choice Awards

Hey Everyone!

I'm Red Phoenix, an author who also happens to be a submissive in real life. I wrote the Brie's Submission series because I wanted people everywhere to know just how much fun BDSM can be.

There is a huge cast of characters who are part of Brie's journey. The further you read into the story the more you learn about each one. I hope you grow to love Brie and the gang as much as I do.

They've become like family.

When I'm not writing, you can find me online with readers.

I heart my fans! ~Red

To find out more visit my Website
redphoenixauthor.com
Follow Me on BookBub
bookbub.com/authors/red-phoenix
Newsletter: Sign up
redphoenixauthor.com/newsletter-signup
Facebook: AuthorRedPhoenix
Twitter: @redphoenix69
Instagram: RedPhoenixAuthor
I invite you to join my reader Group!
facebook.com/groups/539875076052037

SIGN UP FOR MY NEWSLETTER HERE FOR THE LATEST RED PHOENIX UPDATES

SALES, GIVEAWAYS, NEW RELEASES, EXCLUSIVE SNEAK PEEKS, AND MORE!
SIGN UP HERE
REDPHOENIXAUTHOR.COM/NEWSLETTER-SIGNUP

Red Phoenix is the author of:

Brie's Submission Series:
Teach Me #1
Love Me #2
Catch Me #3
Try Me #4
Protect Me #5
Hold Me #6
Surprise Me #7
Trust Me #8
Claim Me #9
Enchant Me #10
A Cowboy's Heart #11
Breathe with Me #12
Her Russian Knight #13
Under His Protection #14
Her Russian Returns #15
In Sir's Arms #16
Bound by Love #17
Tied to Hope #18
Hope's First Christmas #19
Secrets of the Heart #20

*You can also purchase the AUDIO BOOK **Versions**

Also part of the Submissive Training Center world:

Rise of the Dominates Trilogy
Sir's Rise #1
Master's Fate #2
The Russian Reborn #3

Captain's Duet
Safe Haven #1
Destined to Dominate #2

Other Books by Red Phoenix

Blissfully Undone
* Available in eBook and paperback

(Snowy Fun—Two people find themselves snowbound in a cabin where hidden love can flourish, taking one couple on a sensual journey into ménage à trois)

His Scottish Pet: Dom of the Ages
* Available in eBook and paperback

Audio Book: *His Scottish Pet: Dom of the Ages*

(Scottish Dom—A sexy Dom escapes to Scotland in the late 1400s. He encounters a waif who has the potential to free him from his tragic curse)

The Erotic Love Story of Amy and Troy
* Available in eBook and paperback

(Sexual Adventures—True love reigns, but fate continually throws Troy and Amy into the arms of others)

eBooks

Varick: The Reckoning

(Savory Vampire—A dark, sexy vampire story. The hero navigates the dangerous world he has been thrust into with lusty passion and a pure heart)

Keeper of the Wolf Clan (Keeper of Wolves, #1)

(Sexual Secrets—A virginal werewolf must act as the clan's mysterious Keeper)

The Keeper Finds Her Mate (Keeper of Wolves, #2)

(Second Chances—A young she-wolf must choose between old ties or new beginnings)

The Keeper Unites the Alphas (Keeper of Wolves, #3)

(Serious Consequences—The young she-wolf is captured by the rival clan)

Boxed Set: Keeper of Wolves Series (Books 1-3)

(Surprising Secrets—A secret so shocking it will rock Layla's world. The young she-wolf is put in a position of being able to save her werewolf clan or becoming the reason for its destruction)

Socrates Inspires Cherry to Blossom

(Satisfying Surrender—A mature and curvaceous woman becomes fascinated by an online Dom who has much to teach her)

By the Light of the Scottish Moon

(Saving Love—Two lost souls, the Moon, a werewolf, and a death wish…)

In 9 Days

(Sweet Romance—A young girl falls in love with the new student, nicknamed "the Freak")

9 Days and Counting

(Sacrificial Love—The sequel to *In 9 Days* delves into the emotional reunion of two longtime lovers)

And Then He Saved Me

(Saving Tenderness—When a young girl tries to kill herself, a man of great character intervenes with a love that heals)

Play With Me at Noon

(Seeking Fulfillment—A desperate wife lives out her fantasies by taking five different men in five days)

Connect with Red on Substance B

Substance B is a platform for independent authors to directly connect with their readers. Please visit Red's Substance B page where you can:

- Sign up for Red's newsletter
- Send a message to Red
- See all platforms where Red's books are sold

Visit Substance B today to learn more about your favorite independent authors.